Traci Douglass is a *USA TODAY* bestselling author of contemporary and paranormal romance. Her stories feature sizzling heroes full of dark humour, quick wit and major attitude, and heroines who are smart, tenacious, and always give as good as they get. She holds an MFA in Writing Popular Fiction from Seton Hill University, and she loves animals, chocolate, coffee, hot British actors and sarcasm—not necessarily in that order.

Also by Traci Douglass

Discover more at millsandboon.co.uk.

THEIR HOT HAWAIIAN FLING

TRACI DOUGLASS

MILLS & BOON

Published in Great Britain 2020
by Mills & Boon, an imprint of HarperCollins*Publishers*
1 London Bridge Street, London, SE1 9GF

ISBN: 978-0-263-08752-9

MIX
Paper from
responsible sources
FSC® C007454

This book is produced from independently certified FSC™ paper
to ensure responsible forest management.
For more information visit www.harpercollins.co.uk/green.

Printed and bound in Great Britain
by CPI Group (UK) Ltd, Croydon, CR0 4YY

May there always be warmth in your Hale,
fish in your net,
and Aloha in your heart.

Traditional Hawaiian Blessing

CHAPTER ONE

"SIR, CAN YOU tell me your name?" Dr. Leilani Kim asked as she shone a penlight to check her newest patient's eyes. "Pupils equal and reactive. Sir, do you remember what happened? Can you tell me where you are?"

"Get that thing outta my face," the man said, squinting, his words slightly slurred from whatever substance currently flooded his system. "I ain't telling you my name. I know my rights."

"How many fingers am I holding up?" she asked.

"Four." He scowled. "How many am I holding up?"

She ignored his rude gesture and grabbed the stethoscope around her neck to check his vitals. "Pulse 110. Breathing normal. Blood pressure?"

"One-thirty over 96, Doc," one of the nurses said from the other side of the bed.

"Find any ID at the accident scene?" Leilani asked over her shoulder to the EMTs standing near the door of the trauma bay. "Any idea what he's on?"

"Cops got his license," one of the EMTs said, a young woman name Janet. "His name's Greg Chambers. According to the officer who ran his plates, he has a history of DUIs and a couple arrests for meth too."

"Great." It wasn't, in fact, great. It was exhausting

and brought up a lot of memories Leilani would just as soon forget, but that wouldn't be professional, and she couldn't afford to seem anything but perfect these days with the Emergency Medicine directorship up for grabs.

A quick check for signs of distress on the guy—airway, breathing, circulation—all seemed intact and normal. Next, she moved to palpate the patient's torso and extremities. "Do you have pain anywhere other than your head, Mr. Chambers? Can you feel your arms and legs?"

"I feel you poking and prodding me, if that's what you mean." The guy groaned and raised a hand to the bandages covering his scalp. "My head hurts."

"Smashing it into a windshield will do that," Leilani said, finding no evidence of broken bones or internal bleeding on exam. She returned to his head wound. He was lucky. If only the people Leilani had loved most in the world had been so fortunate.

She blinked hard against the unwanted prickle of tears. Must be the exhaustion. Had to be. She never let her personal feelings interfere with her duties.

"Everything okay, Doc?" Pam, the nurse, asked while adjusting the patient's heart monitor.

"Fine. Thanks." Leilani gave her a curt nod, then turned to the paramedics again. "Any other casualties from the accident?"

"Other than the palm tree he hit at forty miles per hour?" Peter, the other EMT, said. "No. No other passengers or vehicles involved, thank goodness. When we arrived, the patient was standing outside his vehicle, texting on his phone. He took one look at us and complained of neck pain before collapsing on the ground claiming he couldn't stand."

"Where's my truck?" Mr. Chambers grumbled.

"Your vehicle is a total loss, sir," Leilani said, hackles rising. People died because idiots like this guy drove under the influence. She checked the laceration on his head.

"No!" He wrenched his arm away from the phlebotomist who'd arrived to take his blood. "You can't take it without my consent. I know my rights."

Energy and patience running low, Leilani fixed the man with a pointed stare. "You keep complaining about your rights, Mr. Chambers, but what about the rights of the other people on the road who just wanted to get home to their family and friends? You put innocent lives at risk driving while intoxicated. What about *their* rights?"

His chin jutted out. "Not my problem."

It will be, if your test results come back positive, she thought, but didn't say it out loud.

Leilani had dealt with her share of belligerent patients during her ten years working at Honolulu's Ohana Medical Center, but this guy took the cake. She turned to Pam. "Call radiology and see if they can get him in for a stat skull X-ray, please. Also, we need a Chem Seven, tox screen and blood alcohol level." Then, to the phlebotomist, "Strap his arm down if needed."

"I'm no addict," the guy yelled, trying to get up and setting off the alarms on the monitors. "Let me out of here."

Several orderlies stepped forward to hold the guy down as Leilani recorded her findings in the patient's file on her tablet.

"How much have you had to drink tonight, sir?" she asked, glancing up.

"Few beers," the patient said, shrugging.

The scent of booze had been heavy on his breath, and Leilani raised a skeptical brow. Based on his delayed reaction times during her exam and his uncoordinated movements, he'd had way more than he was letting on. "And?"

"A couple shots of whiskey."

"And?"

His lips went thin.

Right. Her simmering anger notched higher. The fact someone could be so reckless as to get behind the wheel when they were obviously impaired sent a fresh wave of furious adrenaline through her.

Movements stiff with tension, she set her tablet aside and returned to the bandages on the guy's forehead, peeling them back to reveal a large bruise and several small cuts. She dictated her findings as she went. "On exam there are no obvious skull fractures. Several small lacerations to the forehead and a golf-ball-sized hematoma over the left eye. No obvious foreign bodies seen in the wounds, though we'll need the X-rays to confirm. Sutures aren't necessary, but Pam, can you please clean and dress this again." She glanced over at the EMTs once more. "You said he hit the windshield?"

"Glass starred from the impact."

"Okay. Let's examine your spine next, Mr. Chambers."

"No." He attempted to climb off the bed again. "I want to go home."

"You're not going anywhere until I sign the discharge papers and the police release you from custody," Leilani said, leveraging her weight to hold her uncooperative patient down. People always assumed because she was petite she couldn't handle it if things got rough. What those same folks didn't know was that she was an excellent kickboxer and had already survived way more hardship than most people faced in a lifetime. She was more than capable of fighting her own battles.

"Cops? Aw. Hell. No." The patient gave Leilani a quick once-over. "What are you, ten?"

"Thirty-four, actually." She opened his brace with one hand and carefully palpated his neck with the other, moving her fingers along his spine before cupping his head and turning it slowly from side to side. "No step-offs. Pam please order a stat spinal series as well, since he complained of difficulty walking at the accident scene. Mr. Chambers, were you wearing a seat belt at the time of the accident?"

"Nah. Don't like them. Too confining."

That was kind of the point. Seat belts saved lives. She was proof.

The phlebotomist finished drawing her last vial of blood, then placed a bandage on the patient's arm. "I'll get this right up to the lab, Dr. Kim."

"Thanks." Leilani picked up her tablet once more. "Patient has a possible concussion and will need observation for the next twenty-four hours. Pam, make sure the jail can accommodate that order."

"Will do, Doc," Pam said.

"I ain't going to jail," Mr. Chambers snarled.

"The police might think differently. You caused quite a bit of property damage, from what I've been told, and this isn't your first offense." Leilani rubbed the nape of her neck, her fingers brushing over the scar there. Twenty years since the accident that had changed her life forever, but the memories still brought a fresh wave of pain.

"Police are ready to question the patient whenever you're finished, Dr. Kim," Pam said, hiking her head toward the two uniformed officers standing just outside the door.

"Okay." Leilani turned back to the patient. "Almost done, Mr. Chambers. Just a few more questions."

"Not saying another word," the man said, his scowl dark. "Told you I know my rights."

"Anything I can help with, Dr. Kim?" a new voice said, deep and distracting as hell.

Leilani turned to see Dr. Holden Ross wedging his way between the cops and into the room as Pam was leaving to call in her orders. Ugh. Just what she didn't need. The ER's new locum tenens trauma surgeon barging into her case uninvited. He'd only been here a month, so perhaps he didn't know any better, but it still irked her. She didn't do well with people overstepping her boundaries. She'd worked hard to put up those walls over the years, both professionally and personally. Letting people too close only meant a world of hurt and trouble when they left. And in Leilani's experience, everyone left eventually. Sometimes with no warning at all.

The fact his gorgeous smile filled her stomach with anxious butterflies had nothing to do with it.

She straightened and smoothed her hand down the front of her white lab coat, giving him a polite smile to cover her annoyance. "No. I've got it, thank you, Dr. Ross. Just finishing up."

"Got something you can finish up right here, darlin'." The patient shot her a lewd look and grabbed his crotch.

How charming. Not.

Holden's expression quickly sharpened as he moved to the patient's bedside, his limp drawing her attention once more. She wondered what had caused it before she could stop herself, though it was none of her business. His metal cane clinked against the bedside rails as he glared down into the drunken man's face, his stern frown brimming with warning. "Show Dr. Kim some respect. She's here to save your life."

"I appreciate your concern, Dr. Ross," Leilani said, clearing her throat. "But I've got this. I'm sure there are other patients for you to deal with."

"Actually, I'm just coming on shift." He leaned back, his gaze still locked on the patient. "Fill me in on this guy, so I can take over after you leave."

Darn. He was right. Her shift was over soon, and she needed to get home and rest. Leilani looked over at her colleague again. Holden looked as fresh and bright as a new penny, while she probably looked as ragged as she felt. Add in the fact she seemed irrationally aware of his presence today—not just as a colleague, but as a man—and her stress levels skyrocketed.

The last thing she needed right now was an ill-advised attraction to her coworker.

Distracted, Leilani turned away to futz with her tablet. "What time is it now?"

"Quarter past six," Holden said, moving around the bed to stand next to her. He propped a hip against the edge of the counter, using his cane to take the weight off his right leg. "Your shift ended fifteen minutes ago."

The low hum of the automatic blood pressure cuff inflating on the patient's arm filled the silence. Gossip was already flying amongst the staff about how handsome, intriguing Dr. Ross had ended up at Ohana. Everything from a bad breakup to a good recommendation from some powerful donors. There was one rumor, however, that concerned Leilani the most—that he'd come to their facility at the request of the hospital's chief administrator, Dr. Helen King, and that he was in line for the same directorship she wanted.

Ugh. She shook off the thoughts. None of that mattered at present. She had a patient to deal with. Plus, it was silly to operate off rumor and conjecture. She was a woman of science; she dealt with facts and figures, concrete ideas. Nothing silly or scary like gossip or emotions. Acting on "what-if's" and messy feelings could bring a person to their knees if they weren't careful. Leilani should know.

Pam poked her head into the room again. "Sorry to interrupt, but Dr. Ross, there's a new arrival for you. Female with abdominal pain for the last six hours."

"Duty calls." Holden held Leilani's gaze a moment longer before pushing away from the counter to scan the tablet computer Pam handed him. Leilani found herself unable to stop watching him, darn it. Her curiosity about him was a mystery. Sure, he was charming and would've been just her type, with those dark good looks and soulful hazel eyes. Not to mention he was more than competent at his job, according to the residents on staff. Neither of those reasons was good enough to go poking around into things that were better left unexplored though. Besides, Dr. Ross would hopefully be gone once a suitable replacement for his position was found. Leilani's life was here, in her native Hawaii, and right now her attention was on her career.

There'd be plenty of time for a personal life later.
Maybe.
Shaking off the odd pang of loneliness pinching her

chest, she continued to complete her documentation while Holden rattled off his orders for Pam.

"Okay. Let's start by running an HCG to make sure the new patient's not pregnant, since she's not had a hysterectomy," Holden said, tapping his tablet screen several more times. "I've added a couple of additional tests as well to get things rolling."

"Thanks, Dr. Ross." Pam took the tablet and disappeared around the corner once more, leaving just the two of them and the patient in the trauma bay again.

Leilani stayed determined to power on through because that's what she did. She was a survivor, in more ways than one. She swallowed hard and rubbed her neck again. The scars reminded her how life could change in a second. There was no time to waste.

Her patient's snores filled the air and she shook the man gently awake. "Mr. Chambers? Can you tell me where you are?"

He squinted his eyes open and scrunched his nose. "Why are you asking me this crap?"

"Because you could have a concussion." She glanced over at Holden and gave a resigned sigh. He obviously wasn't going to leave until she shared the case details with him. Seemed he was as stubborn as she was. Not a good sign. After another resigned sigh, she ran through the details for him. "Single car MVA. Male, twenty-six years old, drove his pickup truck into a tree. Head struck windshield. Denies lack of consciousness. He's alert and—"

"Let me go, dammit!" The patient flailed on the bed and clawed at the neck brace. "Get this thing off me!"

"Combative," Leilani finished, giving Holden a look before returning her attention to Mr. Chambers. "Sir, tell me where you are, and I'll get you something for the pain."

He rattled off the hospital's name, then held out his hand. "Where's my OxyContin?"

"Acetaminophen on the way," she countered, typing the order into her tablet and hitting Send.

"Hell no." The patient struggled to sit up again. "Opioids. That's what I want."

Holden stepped nearer to the patient's bedside again, his face pale. "Calm down, sir."

"Go to hell!" The patient kicked hard, his foot making hard contact with Holden's right thigh.

Holden cursed under his breath and grabbed his leg, "What's he on?"

"Not sure yet. Definitely alcohol, but probably drugs too. Waiting on the tox screen results," Leilani said, scanning her chart notes for an update and finding none yet. "Patient has a hematoma on his forehead and a few lacerations, as you can see. No palpable fractures to the neck or spine, no internal bleeding or injuries upon exam, though I've ordered X-rays to confirm. According to the EMTs, his head starred the windshield, so no air bags either. I'd guess the vehicle was too old."

"Before 1999, then," Holden murmured as he rubbed his thigh and winced.

"Before 1998," Leilani corrected him. "Air bags were required in 1998."

"Sorry to disagree, Dr. Kim, but I researched this during my time in Chicago. Air bags became mandatory in 1999 in the United States."

"Then your research was wrong." Leilani battled a rising tide of annoyance as her grip on her tablet tightened. She of all people should know when air bags became mandatory. The date was seared in her mind for eternity. "It was 1998. Trust me."

"Why are we even arguing about this?" he asked, the irritation in his voice matching her own.

"I'm not arguing. I'm correcting you."

"That would be fine if I was mistaken. Which I'm not."

"I beg to differ. The date was September 1, 1998, to be exact."

She squared her shoulders and held her ground, feeling a strange rush of both energy and attraction. No. Not attraction. She didn't want to be attracted to this bullheaded man. Period. Still, her heart raced and her stomach fluttered despite her wishes. Must be the exhaustion. Had to be. She turned away, incensed, both at herself and Dr. Ross.

"The Intermodal Surface Transportation Efficiency Act of 1991 went into effect on September 1, 1998."

Her words emerged in staccato fashion. Rude? Maybe, but then he'd been the one to insinuate himself into her case without asking. She did a quick internet search to prove her point, then held the evidence on screen before his face.

"See? Every truck and car sold in the US had to have air bags for the driver and front seat passenger."

Holden scanned the information, then crossed his arms, the movement causing his toned biceps to bunch. Not that she was looking. Nope. He narrowed his gaze and studied her, far too perceptively for her comfort. "And you know all that verbatim why?"

Because they would've saved the lives of my family.

She swallowed hard and turned away, not about to share the most painful secrets of her past with a virtual stranger, even though some odd little niggle inside of her wanted to.

Gah! She must be way more tired than she'd originally thought. Sleep. That was what she needed. Sleep and food, because perhaps her blood sugar was low. That could explain her stumbling heart rate. Perhaps could even explain how she seemed hypersensitive to the heat and nearness of him now as they faced off over the span of a few feet. Might also explain her weird sensory hallucinations, like how the scent of his skin—soap and musk—seemed to surround her. Or the way her fingertips itched to touch the shadow of dark stubble just beneath the surface of his taut jaw.

Ugh. Leilani clenched her fists on the countertop, the weight of his stare still heavy behind her. He was waiting on her reply and didn't appear to want to leave until he got it. Fine. No way would she tell him the truth, so she went with a half lie instead. "I watch a lot of documentaries."

"Hmm." He sounded thoroughly unconvinced. "I like those shows too, but that's a lot of random facts to remember for no rea—"

"Radiology's ready for your patient, Dr. Kim," Pam said from the doorway, giving Leilani a much-needed reprieve.

"Thank you," Leilani said as two techs wheeled Mr. Chambers out the door.

Holden still stood there though, watching her closely. "I'll handle him when he's done, Dr. Kim. Go home."

"I'm fine, Dr. Ross." Keeping her gaze averted, Leilani headed for the hallway, thankful to escape. "I've got plenty of paperwork to catch up on before I leave, so I'll still be here to wrap up his case."

* * *

Holden couldn't understand the enigma that was Dr. Leilani Kim and it bothered him.

Figuring people out was kind of his thing these days. Or at least attempting to understand what made them work, before they did something completely unexpected, like shoot up a room full of innocent people.

Frustrated, he ran a hand through his hair before heading down the hall to check on his abdominal pain patient. Each step sent a fresh jolt of pain through his nerve endings, thanks to that kick from Dr. Kim's patient.

He stopped at the nurses' station to grab his tablet and give his right leg a rest. Honestly, he shouldn't complain about the pain, since he was lucky to still be breathing, let alone walking, after an attacker's bullet had shattered his right femur and nicked his femoral artery. He could have just as easily bled out on the floor of that Chicago ER, same as David…

No.

Thinking about that now would only take away his edge and he needed to stay sharp, with a twenty-four-hour shift looming ahead of him. Bad enough he still had that argument with Dr. Kim looping through his head. There was something about her excuse for knowing all those obscure facts about air bags that didn't ring true. And sure, he loved documentaries as much as the next person—in fact, those things were like crack to an analytical nerd like himself—but even he couldn't recite back all the information he'd learned in those films word for word like she had. It was odd. And intriguing. He'd had a good reason for discovering all that information, namely for an article he'd written for a medical journal. But her?

Not that he should care why she knew. And yet, he did. Way more than he should.

Irritated as much with himself as with her, he shook his head and pulled up his new patient's file. The last thing he needed in his life was more puzzles. He already had more than enough to figure out. Like where he planned to live after his stint here in Hawaii was done. Like if he'd ever walk without a cane again. Like when the next attack might occur and if he'd be ready this time or if he'd become just another statistic on the news.

The area around the nurses' station grew more crowded and Holden moved down the hall toward his patient's room and open space. He didn't do well with crowds these days. Preferred to keep to himself mostly, do his work, handle his cases, stay safe, stay out of the way and out of trouble. That was what he focused on most of the time. Which is what made his choice to charge into Dr. Kim's trauma bay so strange. Usually, he wouldn't intrude in another colleague's case unless he'd been called for a consult, but then he'd overheard her arguing with her obviously intoxicated patient and something had smacked him hard in the chest, spurring him into that room before he'd even realized what he was doing.

Holden exhaled slowly and dug the tip of his cane into the shiny linoleum floor. His therapist back in Chicago probably would've said it was related to his anxiety from the shooting. After all, the gunman back in Chicago had been intoxicated too. He'd wanted opioids, just like Dr. Kim's patient was demanding. There was a major difference this time though. No firearm.

He took another deep breath. Yes. That had to be it. Had to explain his weird fascination with finding out more about Dr. Leilani Kim too. The fact she was beautiful, all dark hair and dark eyes and curves for days on end—exactly his type, if he'd been looking—had nothing to do with it.

He definitely wasn't looking.

It was simply the stress of being in a new place, and his posttrauma hypersensitivity to his surroundings. He'd only been here a month, after all. Yep. That was it. Never mind his instincts told him otherwise. Holden didn't trust his instincts. Hadn't for a year now.

Twelve months had passed since the attack on his ER in Chicago. Twelve months since he'd lost his best friend in a senseless act of violence. Twelve months since he'd failed to keep the people closest to him safe.

And why risk getting closer to anyone again when they could be lost so easily?

The tablet pinged with his patient's results and he pulled them up, scrolling through the data. Pregnancy test negative. White blood cell count normal, though that didn't necessarily rule out appendicitis. Amylase and lipase measurements within normal limits. Next steps—an ultrasound and manual exam.

"Hey, Pam?" he called down the hall. "Can you join me in Trauma Three for a pelvic?"

"Yep, just give me a sec to finish up calling the lab for Dr. Kim," she said, holding her hand over the phone receiver.

He nodded, then leaned a shoulder against the wall to wait. Ohana Medical Center was relatively quiet, compared to the busy downtown ER he'd come from in Chicago. Back then he'd loved the constant hustle, but after the shooting, going back to work there had been too painful. So, he'd chosen the locum tenens route instead. And it was that choice that had eventually reunited him with his old friend, Dr. Helen King. In fact, she was the reason he'd ended up at Ohana. He owed her a debt he could never repay, but he'd wanted to try.

Which explained why he was here, in the middle of paradise, wondering how soon he could leave. Staying in one place too long didn't suit him anymore. Staying put meant risking entanglements. Staying put too long made you vulnerable.

And if there was one thing Holden never wanted to be again, it was vulnerable.

A loud metal clang sounded down the hall and his senses immediately went on high alert, his mind throwing up reminders of a different ER, a different, dangerous situation. His best friend lying on the floor, bleeding out and Holden unable to stop it because of his own injuries. His chest squeezed tight and darkness crept into his peripheral vision as the anxiety took over.

No. Not here. Not now. Can't do this. Won't do this.

Pulse jackhammering and skin prickling, Holden turned toward the corner, trying to look busy so no one questioned why he was just standing there alone in the hall. He'd spent weeks after the attack learning how to cope with the flashbacks, the PTSD. Sometimes the shadows still won though, usually when he was tired or anxious. Considering he'd slept like crap the night before, he was both at the moment.

"Sorry for the holdup," Pam said, near his side and breaking through his jumbled thoughts. "Things are a bit crazy right now, with tourist season and all."

He nodded and hazarded a glance in her direction.

Her smile quickly dissolved into a frown at whatever she saw in his face. "You okay, Doc?"

It took him a moment to recover his voice, his response emerging more like a croak past his dry vocal cords. "Fine." He cleared his throat and tried again, forcing a smile he didn't quite feel. "Isn't it always tourist season in Hawaii?"

"It is," said another voice from the staff break room across the hall. Leilani. Crap. He'd been so distracted he'd not even seen her go in there. Adrenaline pounded through his blood. Had she seen his panic attack?

When she came out of the room though, she thankfully gave no indication she'd seen him acting strangely. She just walked past him and headed for the elevators as radiology wheeled out her inebriated patient.

The lingering tension inside Holden ratcheted higher as the patient continued to shout at the staff while they wheeled him back toward the trauma bay. "Pain meds! Now!"

Leilani headed behind the desk at the nurses' station once more. "Let me check the images."

Holden followed behind her, the pain in his leg taking a back seat to his need to prevent a possible calamity if her patient got out of hand again. He reached the nurses' station just as Dr. Kim pulled up the patient's images on the computer. "No embedded glass in his scalp, cervical vertebra appear normal. No damage to the spinal cord or—"

"I'm getting the hell out of here!" A jarring rip of Velcro sounded, followed by a resounding crack of plastic hitting the floor. "And I will take everyone down if I don't get my meds!"

The cops still waiting near the doorway tensed and Holden's heart lodged in his throat.

Oh God. Not again.

Undeterred, Leilani took off for the patient's room. "Time to get this guy discharged."

"Wait!" Holden grabbed her arm. "Don't go in there."

"That's my patient, Dr. Ross." She frowned, shaking off his hold. "Don't tell me how to do my work. We need that bed and he's cleared for discharge. He's the cops' problem now. Excuse me."

She continued on down the hall, signaling to the officers to follow her into the room.

"I want my OxyContin!" Mr. Chambers yelled, followed by a string of curses.

Holden breathed deeply, forcing himself to stay calm, stay present, stay in control.

This isn't Chicago. This patient doesn't have a gun. There are police officers present. No one will get hurt.

From his vantage point, Holden saw the patient sitting up on the side of the bed, his neck brace on the floor. Leilani approached slowly, her voice low and calm.

"Your X-rays were all negative. We're going to release you into police custody."

"Already told you," the patient said, teetering to his feet. "I ain't talking to no cops."

Time seemed to slow as Holden moved forward, his vision blurring with memories of the shooting. So much blood, so much chaos, so much wasted time and energy and life.

Breathe, man. Breathe.

The patient straightened, heading straight for Dr. Kim. The cops moved closer.

Her tone hardened. "I'd advise you to stay where you are for your own safety, sir."

"My safety?" The patient sneered. "You threatening me?"

"Not a threat." Leilani squared her shoulders. "Touching me would not be wise."

"Wise?" The guy snorted, his expression lascivious. "C'mon and gimme some sugar."

The cops placed their hands on their Tasers, saying in unison, "Stand down, sir."

Holden rushed toward the room, his cane creaking under the strain. He couldn't let this happen again, not on his watch. He couldn't fail, wouldn't fail.

Just as Holden shoved between the officers, the patient turned at the sudden commotion and swung. His fist collided hard with Holden's jaw and pain surged through his teeth. He stumbled backward. The cops pulled their Tasers as the patient grabbed Dr. Kim's ponytail. Fast as lightning, she swiveled to face Mr. Chambers, slamming her heel down on his instep until his grip on her hair loosened. Then, as he bent over and cursed, she kneed him twice in the groin. The guy crumbled to the ground and the cops took him into custody.

Over. It's over.

Holden slumped against the wall as time sped back to normal.

While the cops handcuffed Mr. Chambers and read him his rights, Leilani rushed to Holden's side. "You're bleeding."

Confused, he glanced down at his scrub shirt and saw a large splotch of scarlet. Then the ache in his jaw and teeth intensified, along with the taste of copper and salt in his mouth.

Damn.

"Here." Leilani snatched a few gauze pads from a canister on the counter and handed them to him. "Looks like there's a pretty deep gash on your lip and chin." She leaned past him to call out into the hall. "Pam, can you set up an open room for suturing, please?"

"No, no." He attempted to bat her hands away and straightened. "I can stitch myself up."

He was a board-certified trauma surgeon, for God's sake. Though as the adrenaline in his system burned away, it left him feeling a tad shaky. His lip pulsated with pain. At least it was a welcome distraction from the cramp in his thigh. "Seriously, I've got it."

"Don't be silly. It will be easier for someone else to stitch you up." She tugged him out the door and down the hall to the nurses' station once more. "Just let me sign off on Mr. Chambers first so they can get him out of here."

While he waited, he blotted his throbbing mouth with the gauze pads and admitted she was right, much as he hated to do so. He was in no fit state to treat anyone at the moment, including himself. Which brought another problem to mind. "What about the abdominal patient?"

"Let the residents take it. That's why they're here." Leilani finished her signing off on her discharge paperwork, then nudged Holden toward an empty exam room. Behind him, the cops hauled Mr. Chambers, still cursing and yelling, out to their waiting squad car.

Leilani led him into the room Pam had set up, then shut the door behind them. "Take a seat on the exam table and let me take a look at your lip."

He did as she asked, allowing her to brush his hand aside and peek beneath the gauze pad. This close, her warmth surrounded him, as did her scent—jasmine and lily. A strange tingle in his blood intensified. It was far more unsettling and dangerous than any punch to the face. She moved closer still to examine his cut lip and he jerked away, alarmed.

"Don't!" he said, then tried to backpedal at her concerned look. "I mean, *ow.*"

He turned away and she walked over to the suture kit set out along with a small vial of one percent lidocaine and a syringe on a wheeled metal tray. "The spilt is through the vermillion border, so no Dermabond or Steri-Strips. Sutures will give you the best result—otherwise it could pop open again."

Holden stared at his reflection in the mirror nearby to distract himself, frustration and embarrassment curdling within him. He already felt like an idiot after getting punched by her patient. Having her sew him up too added insult to injury. Pain surged through his leg and he gripped the edge of the table.

"Any dizziness?" Leilani asked. "He hit you pretty hard."

"No," Holden lied. He still felt a bit light-headed, but that was more from anxiety than the blow to his face. Needing to burn off some excess energy, he slid off the table and moved to the nearby sink to splash cold water on his face. The chill helped clear his head and after drying off his face with paper towels, he plucked at his soiled scrub shirt. "I should change."

"Hang on." Leilani ran back out into the hall and returned with a clean scrub shirt a few moments later. "Here."

"Thanks." He limped behind the screen in the corner and stripped, tossing the bloodstained shirt on the floor before slipping on the clean one. It was too big and the

V-neck kept slipping to the side, revealing the scar from his second bullet wound through his left shoulder. He fiddled with the stupid thing, glancing up to find Leilani watching him in the mirror on the wall.

He attempted to play off the awkwardness of the situation with a joke. "Checking me out?"

"No." She looked away fast, but not before he spotted a flush of pink across her cheeks. His interest in her spiked again, despite his wishes to the contrary. She was his work colleague. Theirs was a professional relationship, pure and simple. Anything more was definitely off-limits. He made his way back to the exam table as she pulled on a pair of gloves, then filled a syringe with lidocaine.

"People can be unpredictable, can't they?" Leilani said, jarring him back to reality. "Like Mr. Chambers. You think they're going to do one thing, then they do something completely different. Lie down, please." Reluctantly, he did as she asked. The sooner they got this over with, the better.

Leilani moved in beside him again and he did his best to ignore the heat of her penetrating through his cotton scrub shirt, the soft brush of her bare wrist against his skin as she stabilized his jaw for the injection. "Hold still and try to relax. This may burn a bit."

"I know." He did his best to relax and met her intent stare. "Hard being on the receiving end of treatment."

She smiled and his pulse stumbled. "I understand, Dr. Ross. Doctors usually make the worst patients." She leaned back, her gaze darting from his eyes to his left shoulder, then back again. "But you've obviously had treatment before."

He swallowed hard and looked away, anxiety still

shimmering like hot oil through his bloodstream. "Obviously."

"Sorry. I didn't mean to bring up a sore subject." Her hand slipped from his jaw to rest on his sternum, her smile falling. "You're tachycardic."

"I'm fine," he repeated, grasping her hand, intending to remove it from his person, but once her fingers were in his, he found himself unable to let go. Which was nuts. He didn't want entanglements, didn't want connections, and yet, here it was—in the last place he wanted to find one. Which only made his heart beat harder against his rib cage.

Get it together, man.

"Dr. Ross?" she asked, concern lighting her gaze. "Holden? Are you with me?"

The unfamiliar sound of his first name on her lips returned a modicum of his sanity. "Sorry. No, I'd rather not talk about my injuries. Bad memories."

"Okay. No problem. I understand completely. I have a few of those memories myself." Her calm tone, along with the understanding in her eyes, slowly brought his inner angst down to tolerable levels. She pulled her hand from his, then walked over to her tablet on the counter and tapped the screen. "How about some music? What kind do you like? Rock? Country? R & B?"

The change of subjects provided a welcome escape and he grabbed on to it with both hands. He stared up at the ceiling and couldn't care less what she played, as long as it distracted him from the past and her weird effect on him. "Uh…whatever you like is fine."

"Okay." Ukulele music filled the air as she moved in beside him again, a twinkle in her dark gaze as she raised the syringe once more. "I know this situation is uncomfortable for you, Dr. Ross, but the sooner you let me get started, the faster it will be over. I'll even make you a deal. Let me suture you up and I'll take you to a real luau."

"What?" He frowned up at her.

"A luau. You know, poi, Kalua pig, poke, *lomi* salmon, *opihi, haupia* and beer. The works. Plus, you might even get to see a genuine Don Ho impersonator."

"Um…a genuine impersonator?" He gave her a confused look.

She laughed. "Yep. He's the best on the island. Be a shame for you not to get the full Hawaiian experience while you're here. Unless you've already been?"

No. He hadn't been to a luau yet. Hadn't really been anywhere on the island, other than the resort where he was staying and the hospital, to be honest. And sure, he'd planned to take in some sights while he was here, of course, including a luau, but he'd not really made any firm decisions. The fact she'd asked him now, both piqued his interest and set off all the warning bells in his head. "Are you asking me out on a date, Dr. Kim?"

"What?" She stepped back, looking nearly as alarmed as he felt. "No. I just felt bad because my patient punched you and wanted to make you more comfortable, that's all." That pretty pink color was back in her cheeks again, and damn if that unwanted interest in her didn't flare higher.

This was bad. So, so bad.

Luckily, she shrugged and turned away, her tone chilly now. "But I certainly don't want to give you the wrong impression. And I can see now that my asking was a mistake. Forget I mentioned it."

Holden wanted nothing more than to do that, but it

seemed he couldn't. In fact, her invitation now buzzed inside his head like a bothersome fruit fly. He propped himself up on his elbows, feeling completely discombobulated. "I didn't mean to make you uncomfortable."

"Same." She glanced back at him over her shoulder. "I'm not even sure why I mentioned it, to be honest."

The sincerity in her tone helped ease the tension slithering inside him and he lay down flat again, blinking at the ceiling. Seemed they were both rusty at this whole social interaction thing. "I haven't really seen anything since I've been on the island."

"I can give you some suggestions, if you like, since Honolulu's my hometown. My parents own a hotel here," she said, returning to his side, her gaze narrowed as she took his chin again and lifted the syringe. "Okay, here comes the burn."

While the numbing medication took effect, Holden found himself reconsidering her offer. His therapist had told him during their last session back in Chicago that he needed to get out more. She could show him around, perhaps introduce him to some people, broaden his horizons. On a strictly professional basis, of course. Plus, spending more time with her should help lessen the strange heightened awareness he felt around her. Desensitization 101. Taken in those terms, accepting Leilani's invitation made good sense. He blurted out his response before he could second-guess himself. "Okay."

"Okay what?" She frowned down at him.

"Okay, we can go to a luau." His words started to slur as the medication took effect, making his bottom lip ineffective. "Show me some sights too, if you have the time."

Dr. Kim blinked down at him, looking as stunned

as he felt. She seemed to consider it for a long moment before nodding. "Fine. But only as colleagues. Understood?"

He nodded, then exhaled slowly as he tapped his lip to make sure it was numb.

"Good." Her quick smile brightened the room far more than he wished. "Now, no more talking until I get this done. Otherwise, I can't guarantee this will heal symmetrical."

She got to work and he closed his eyes, the better to block her out. He still couldn't quite believe he'd said yes to her invitation. Part of him still wanted to get up and get the heck out of there, but the other part of him knew she was right. It was easier for someone else to stitch him up.

CHAPTER TWO

LEILANI STILL COULDN'T quite believe what had happened
with Holden Ross. What had she been thinking, offering
to take him sightseeing, let alone to a luau? Ugh. She
didn't date coworkers. Didn't date anyone really these
days, truth be told. Sure, she'd had relationships in the
past, but nothing that had worked out long term. And
the past six months or so, socializing had taken a back
seat with the directorship position on the line.

But this wasn't really socializing, was it? He was new
in town and she was being hospitable, that's all.

Like a good neighbor.

A neighbor you'd like to get to know a whole lot better.

Flustered, Leilani turned to face the counter.

This was so not like her to get all giddy over a man.
Especially a potential rival for the job she wanted. Never
mind there was something wildly compelling about him.
Like the flash of panic in his eyes when she'd asked
about his previous injuries.

Unfortunately, his reaction was all too relatable—the
gut-wrenching terror, the uncertainty of being bruised
and battered and broken and alone. If it hadn't been
for the kindness and patience and fast thinking of the

medical staff the night of the accident, she wouldn't be here today.

The old injury at the base of her neck ached again, reminding her of those who'd saved her, after the rest of her family had been lost. And that was probably exactly why she should be avoiding Holden Ross like the proverbial plague, instead of escorting him around her island as his tour guide. Maybe she could find some way out of it. Work usually gave ample excuses. There was bound to be a case or two requiring her assistance, right? Leilani ripped open the suture kit and pulled out a hemostat.

The music streaming from her tablet on the counter switched to a different song, this one slow and sweet and filled with yearning. Her own chest pinched slightly before she shoved the feeling away. She had nothing to yearn for. She had a great life. A good career. Adoptive parents who loved her and supported her decisions. A new house. A pet who adored her—U'i, her African gray parrot.

And sure, maybe sometimes she wished for someone special to share it all with. She'd get there when she was ready.

If you're ever ready...

She was taking her time, that was all. Being cautious. Never mind she still woke up with nightmares from the accident sometimes. She'd get over it. All of it.

Someday.

"No one told me you're a ninja," Holden said, his words wonky due to his numb lip.

"Those skills come in handy more often than you know." She opened a 6–0 suture and grabbed the curved needle with the hemostat to align the vermillion border with one stitch. Once that was done, she switched to a 5–0 absorbable suture for the rest. "Just four or five more then we're done."

"Internal?" he asked, though the word came out more like "ee-turtle."

"No damage to the orbicularis oris muscle that I can see, so all external." She tied off another stitch, then grabbed a couple more gauze strips off the tray, soaking them in saline before carefully pulling down his bottom lip. "Let me just check the inside to make sure there aren't more lacerations hidden in there."

The salt water dripped down his chin to the V-neck of his scrub shirt.

"Oops. Sorry." Leilani grabbed a tissue from the tray and dabbed at the wet spot, doing her best not to notice his tanned skin and well-defined muscles. Sudden, unwanted images of her kissing from his neck to collarbone, then down his chest, lower still, made her mouth go dry…

"Dr. Kim?" Holden said, yanking her back to reality.

Oh God.

Mortified, she tossed the tissue back on the tray then gave him a too-bright smile. "Almost finished."

He frowned, then looked away, the movement giving her another glimpse of the scar on his left shoulder. She gave herself a mental shake. His body and his wounds were none of her business. That was the exhaustion talking, making her nerves hum and her curiosity about him soar. She continued with the sutures, berating herself.

Focus, girl. Focus.

The song on her tablet switched again, this time to a sweeping, sexy guitar concerto.

Holden blinked up at the ceiling, looking anywhere but at her. "That's pretty."

"One of my favorites." Leilani tied off another stitch then started on the next.

He waited until she was finished before asking, "Where'd you learn to fight?"

It took her a minute to figure out his slurred question. "Oh. You mean with Mr. Chambers? I kickbox. I've taken classes since I was fifteen."

"Wow." Then, out of the blue, he reached up and cupped her face. Her pulse stumbled.

"What are you doing, Dr. Ross?" she managed to squeak out.

"That guy pulled your hair hard," Holden said, gently tilting her head to the side.

"I'm fine. Really." Her breath hitched at the intensity of his gaze.

Oh goodness.

The romantic music washed around them, and unexpected heat gathered in her core. Not good. Not good at all.

Holden Ross was the last man she should get involved with. He was her colleague. He was strictly off-limits. He was far too tempting for her own good. Any connection she felt to him needed to be severed, any awareness currently scorching her blood needed to be doused. End of story. She couldn't risk allowing him closer.

Can I?

Blood pounded in her ears and forbidden awareness zinged over her skin. She ignored the first and tamped down the last before forcing words past her suddenly dry throat. "Thank you, Dr. Ross. Now, let's finish these stitches and get you on your way."

"Holden," he said.

"I'm sorry?" She held the needle poised over his lip for the last stitch.

"Call me Holden."

"Okay." Leilani placed her thumb on his chin to pull slight tension and her finger along his chiseled jawline to steady her hand.

"So, you're native Hawaiian then?"

"Please try not to speak." She sat back. "And yes. Born and raised. My parents own a resort in town."

She could hear the sadness in her own voice and as perceptive as he was, she had no doubt he'd hear it too. Despite all the love and joy her adopted family had given her, part of her would always miss the ones who'd gone. The pain of the accident had never truly faded. Nor had the fear of losing someone else she cared for. She tied off the last stitch, then sat back with relief. "All done."

He sat up and looked in the mirror on the wall again. "Nice job, Dr. Kim."

"Thanks." She began cleaning up from the procedure. "There are more clean scrub shirts on the rack in the hall, if you want to grab a different size."

"Will do." He grabbed his cane and limped toward the door, then turned back to her once more. "Thanks again."

"No problem." Leilani watched him walk away, feeling that riptide of interest tugging at her again and knowing that if she gave in, it could pull her right under. And drowning in the mysteries of Dr. Holden Ross was not part of her plans.

The following morning, after his shift, Holden drove his rental car through the streets of Honolulu toward the

Malu Huna Resort and Spa, the steady, hypnotic beat of the windshield wipers almost putting him to sleep. His current residence was only fifteen minutes outside of downtown but driving in the rain after work wasn't exactly his favorite thing.

He pulled into a handicapped parking spot near the entrance to the hotel then stared in through the front windows at the breakfast crowd filling the lobby of the resort. The unusual, crappy weather actually suited his mood far better than the cheerful tropical decor inside the place, but if he wanted to get to his room, he had to traverse the maze of tourists and guests filling the tables in the lobby.

After a deep breath, he cut the engine and grabbed his cane, before glancing at himself one last time in the mirror. The numbing medication in his lip had long since worn off and his lower jaw and into his teeth ached. Eating would be a joy for a while. Not that it mattered. He ate his meals alone in his room most of the time anyway, avoiding the other guests. No sense ruining everyone else's time in paradise with his gloomy attitude.

With a sigh, he got out of the car, then hobbled toward the entrance, his head down to keep the rain off his face. The automatic doors swished open and a gust of warm air swept around him, scented with maple and bacon from the food-laden coffers of the all-you-can-eat buffet in the dining room. His traitorous stomach growled, but Holden didn't stop to fill a plate. Just kept his eyes focused on the elevators ahead as he made a beeline through the lobby. Since the shooting, he had a hard time spending long periods with large groups of strangers. He found himself too distracted, always scanning the room for danger.

His therapist back in Chicago had urged him to build up his tolerance slowly. So far, Holden hadn't tried that suggestion out, preferring his own company to constantly being on guard for the next attack.

Weaving through groups of tourists dressed in shorts and T-shirts and sandals, he felt more out of place than ever in his wrinkled scrubs, his name tag from work still pinned crookedly on the front pocket. He excused himself as he sidled by a quartet of women bedecked with leis and sun hats and nearly collided with a potted palm tree for his trouble.

The lobby of the Malu Huna looked like a cross between a *Fantasy Island* fever dream and a Disney movie in Holden's estimation—with its rattan furniture, gauzy white curtains and golden pineapple design inlaid in the shiny tile floor. There was even a parrot behind the front desk, squawking at the people passing by. Holden glanced over at the bird as he waited for his elevator. An African gray, if he wasn't mistaken. One of his roommates back in college had had one. Smart as a whip and quick learners. They'd had to be careful what they said around the bird because it picked up words like crazy, especially the bad ones.

Holden punched the up button again.

"Dr. Ross?" a voice called from across the lobby and his heart sank. The owner.

The elevator dinged and the doors whooshed open.

So close and yet so far.

He considered making a run for it but didn't want to be rude.

Forcing a weary smile, he turned to face the Asian man who bustled over to him from the dining room. The shorter guy beamed up at him now, his brightly colored Hawaiian shirt all but glowing beneath the recessed overhead lighting. "Won't you join us for breakfast?"

Holden glanced at the roomful of people and his stomach twisted hard. "Oh, I'm not really hungry."

Once more, his stomach growled loud, proving him a liar.

The hotel owner raised a skeptical brow, his grin widening. "Your body says otherwise. Please, Dr. Ross? We'd love to show you our hospitality during your stay." He gave Holden a quick once-over. "You look as if you could use a good meal. Come on."

Before he could protest, the man took his arm and guided him across the lobby. Familiar panic vibrated through his bloodstream and he looked over the man's head out the rain-streaked windows toward his car. It was only breakfast. He could do breakfast.

Sit. Eat. Talk.

Except the idea of making conversation with strangers made his spine kink.

Sure, he talked to patients all day long, but that was different. At the hospital, he had a plan, a specific purpose. Those things made it easier to shove his anxiety to the back of his mind. Small talk, however, required interest and energy, both of which Holden was running critically low on at the moment.

A year ago I could talk with anyone, party with the best of them.

But now, postattack, his social skills had vanished, leaving him feeling awkward and weak. He hated feeling weak. Weak meant vulnerable. And vulnerable was something Holden never wanted to be again.

He made one final valiant attempt at escape as the hotel owner dragged him thorough the dining room and a maze of packed tables. "Honestly, I can just order room service. I'm tired and grubby and probably won't make good company anyway, Mr….?"

"Kim," the man said, stopping before a table where two women sat. "Mr. Kim. But you can call me Joe. Please, sit down, Dr. Ross."

"Holden," he mumbled, staring at the woman across the table from him. Dr. Kim stared back, looking about as happy to see him as he was to see her. "Please, call me Holden."

She'd mentioned her parents owned a hotel in town while she'd stitched him up, but he'd been so focused on ignoring her and all the uncomfortable things she made him feel, that he'd let it go in one ear and out the other.

Now he felt like an even bigger idiot than before. "Uh, hello again."

"Hello," she said, fiddling with the napkin in her lap. "Are you going to sit down?"

Sit. Yes. That sounded like a marvelous idea, especially since his thigh was cramping again. With less grace than usual, he pulled out the empty chair and slid into it, stretching out his aching leg as he hooked his cane over the back of his seat.

Mr. Kim, Joe, was still smiling at him, as was the woman beside him, presumably Mrs. Kim.

Trying his best to not flub up again, Holden extended his hand to the older woman. "Dr. Holden Ross. Pleasure to meet you."

"Same." Mrs. Kim's dark gaze darted between Leilani and Holden. "You work with my daughter?"

"Yes. I'm filling in temporarily at Ohana Medical Center." He sat back as a waitress set a glass of water in front of him. "Trauma surgery."

"Excellent," Mrs. Kim said. "You and Leilani must work together a lot then. Funny she's never mentioned you."

Leilani, who was quieter than he'd ever seen her before, stared down at her plate of food. "I'm sure I mentioned him, Mom."

"He'll have the buffet," Joe said to the waitress, ordering for Holden. "And it's on the house."

"Sure thing, Mr. Kim," the waitress said, walking away.

"No, no," Holden protested. "I can get this. My locum tenens position comes with a food allowance, so…"

"Locum tenens?" Mrs. Kim said, leaning closer to him. "Tell me more about that, Dr. Ross. Sounds fascinating."

"Holden, please," he said, eyeing the crowded buffet table nearby and longing for the peace and quiet of his hotel room. "I…uh…"

"Hey, guys." Leilani's calm voice sliced through his panic. "Leave the poor man alone. He's just worked a long shift. He needs coffee and a nap, not the third degree. Right, Dr. Ross?"

He swallowed hard and managed a nod.

Leilani poured him a cup of coffee from the carafe on the table and pushed it toward him. "Busy at the ER?"

"Yeah." Talking about work helped relax him and as he stirred cream and sugar into his cup, he told them about the cases he'd seen and the funny stories he'd heard from the staff and soon he'd even answered the questions the Kim's had asked him without locking up once. The whole time, he found himself meeting Leilani's gaze across the table and marveling at the sense of peace he found there.

Whoa. Don't get carried away there, cowboy.

His peace had nothing to do with Leilani Kim. That was absurd. They barely knew each other. It was the routine—talking about work—that calmed his nerves. Nothing else. Nope.

"Well, this has been fun," Mrs. Kim said once he'd finished, pushing to her feet. "But my husband and I need to get back to work at the front desk."

Joe looked confused for a minute before his wife gave him a pointed look. "Oh right. Yeah. We need to get to work. You kids stay and have fun. Lani, be sure to invite him to the luau next Friday." He shook Holden's hand again. "See you around the resort."

Holden watched them walk away, then turned back to Leilani. "So, this is the resort your family owns?"

"Yes." She gave him a flat look, then cocked her head toward the buffet. "Better get your food before they start tearing the buffet down."

CHAPTER THREE

LEILANI EXHALED SLOWLY as Holden hobbled away toward the food line. If she'd left five minutes earlier, she would've missed her parents trying to play matchmaker again, this time with the last man on earth she should be interested in.

They were colleagues, for goodness' sake. She didn't date people from work.

No matter how intrigued she might be by Holden's tall, dark and damaged persona.

Part of her wanted to get up and leave right then, but manners dictated she stay at least until he returned with his plate. They did have to work together, after all. She didn't want things to be awkward—or more awkward than they already were—between them.

So, she'd wait until he got back to the table, then make her polite excuses and skedaddle. For once, Leilani was grateful for the long shift ahead of her at work. Twenty-four hours to keep her busy and away from dwelling more on her encounter the day before with Holden. But first, she planned to hit the gym for a good martial arts workout.

She rolled her stiff neck, then sipped her water. Even tired as she'd been, her sleep had been restless, her dreams filled with images of dealing with combative, intoxicated Mark Chambers again. Those moments then had quickly blurred into memories of the long-ago accident that had taken the lives of her parents and brother. Mixed in were flashes of Holden, changing his scrub shirt, the scar on his shoulder, the wary look in his warm hazel eyes as she'd stitched up his lip. The rough scrap of stubble on his jaw that she'd felt even through her gloves as she'd held his chin, the clean smell of shampoo from his hair, the throb of his heart beneath her palm as she'd dabbed the saline solution from his chest...

"So," he said, shaking her from her thoughts as he straddled the chair across from her and set a plate of scrambled eggs, toast and bacon on the table in front of him. "You honestly don't have to stay if you don't want to. I can tell you'd like to leave."

Leilani did her best to play it off. "Don't be silly. I just have a busy day ahead."

He sat back as the waitress returned to fill a cup of coffee for him. The server gave Holden a slow smile filled with promise and a strange jab of something stabbed Leilani's chest. Not jealousy, because that would be insane. She had no reason to care if another woman flirted with Holden. He was a coworker, an acquaintance. That was it.

Holden continued to watch her as he stirred cream and sugar into his coffee, his gaze narrowed. His skeptical tone said he saw right through her flimsy excuse. "Well, don't let me keep you. I wouldn't be here either if your dad hadn't dragged me in."

She frowned at him. It was true she'd planned to leave soon enough, but that didn't mean he shouldn't want her to stay. A niggle of stubbornness bored into her gut, and she accepted a refill on her coffee from the waitress. At Holden's raised brow she said, "I've got a few minutes."

He took a huge bite of eggs and lowered his gaze. "Don't stay on my account."

"Are you always this jovial, Dr. Ross?" she snorted.

"No. Most of the time I eat alone in my room," he said, devouring half a piece of bacon before glancing at her again. This time, his stoic expression cracked slightly into the hint of a smile. "Sorry. Out of practice with socializing."

A pang of sympathy went through her before she could tamp it down. Seemed they were in the same boat there. She sipped her coffee while he finished off his plate, then sat back in his seat. ER doctors learned to eat fast, at least in Leilani's experience, since you never knew when you'd be called out for the next emergency. Leilani wasn't sure where he put all that food, since there didn't appear to be an inch of spare flesh on him. A sudden, unwanted flash of him with his shirt off in the exam room flickered through her mind before she shook it off.

Nope. Not going there. Not at all.

With a sigh, she finished the rest of her coffee in one long swallow, then stood. "Right. Well, I really do need to go now. Have a nice rest of your day, Dr. Ross."

Holden wiped his mouth with a napkin, then gave a small nod. "Your shift at the hospital doesn't start until two. It's only 9:00 a.m. now."

"What?" Heat prickled her cheeks as he caught her in a lie. Outrage mixed with embarrassment inside her and came out in her blunt response. "I wasn't aware my schedule was your concern, Dr. Ross."

He downed another swig of coffee. "It's not. Helen mentioned it earlier."

At the reminder of Ohana's head administrator, Leilani's breath caught. Reason number one billion why she shouldn't be spending any more time than was necessary with this man. Not with Holden potentially vying for the same job she wanted. "Dr. King told you my schedule? That seems odd."

"Not really. She mentioned it in relation to some project she wants us both to work on." Leilani opened her mouth to respond, but he held up a hand. "Before you ask, she didn't give me any details yet. Said she wanted to discuss it with you first, as the acting director." He exhaled slowly, his broad shoulders slumping a bit, and he gestured toward her empty chair. "Look, I'm sorry if I was grumpy before. Please, don't rush off on my account. It's actually kind of nice to have someone to talk to besides myself."

Much as she hated to admit it, Leilani felt the same. Sure, she had friends and her parents, but they weren't physicians. She couldn't talk shop with them like she could another doctor. Not that she really planned to discuss cases with Holden Ross, unless a trauma surgeon's skills were needed, but still. Torn between making her escape and being more enticed by his offer than she cared to admit, Leilani slowly took her seat again. "You don't get out much?"

"No. Not since…" Holden's voice trailed off, and that haunted expression ghosted over his face once more before he hid it behind his usual wall of stoicism. He cleared his throat. "Working locum tenens has a lot of advantages, but creating bonds and connections isn't one of them. Maybe that's why I like it so much."

"Wow. That sounds a bit standoffish."

"Not really." He shook his head and frowned down into his cup. "Just smart."

Huh. Leilani sat back and crossed her arms, studying him. Having been through a nightmare herself with the accident, she recognized the signs of past trauma all too well. Something horrible had definitely happened in his past—she just wasn't sure what. Given his limp and the wound she'd spied on his left shoulder, she'd bet money a bullet had been involved. That was certainly enough to ruin anyone's outlook on their fellow humans and relationships.

Before she could ask more though, he shifted his attention to the windows nearby and the gray, overcast day outside. "Does it rain a lot here?"

"Not really," she said, the change in subject throwing her for a second. "But it's March."

"And March means rain?"

"In Honolulu, yes. It's our rainiest month." Leilani held up her hand when a server came around with a coffeepot again. Too much caffeine would upset her stomach. "Why?"

"Just interested in the island." The same waitress from earlier stopped back to remove Holden's dishes and slid a small piece of paper onto the table beside his mug. From what Leilani could see, it had the woman's phone number on it. Holden seemed unfazed, taking the slip and tucking it into the pocket of his scrubs before reaching for the creamer again. The thought of him having a booty call with the server later made Leilani's gut tighten. Which was stupid. He was free to see anyone he liked, as was she. She wasn't a workaholic spinster, no matter what her parents might say to the contrary. Leilani had options when it came to men and dating. She was just picky, that's all. She had standards.

Holden must've caught her watching him because he said, "I promised to check on the waitress's son later. The kid's got what sounds like strep throat."

Uh-huh. Sure.

She managed not to roll her eyes through superhuman strength. His social life was of no concern to her. She flashed him a bland smile. "Nice of you."

He shrugged. "So, what are you rushing off to this morning? If you don't mind me asking."

Her first response was a snarky one that yeah, she did mind. But then she caught a hint of that lonely sadness and wariness in his eyes again and she bit back those words. She didn't want to get friendlier with Holden Ross, but darn if there wasn't something about him that kept her in her seat and coming back for more. She could lie and make up a story, but what was the point? So she went with the truth instead. "I was going to do my daily workout."

"Oh?" Holden perked up a little at that. "I've been meaning to try the hotel gym, but with my crazy schedule at work, haven't made it there yet. Mind if I tag along, just to see where it is? Then I'll leave you alone, I promise."

Alarm bells went off in Leilani's head. She already felt way more interested in this guy than was wise. Spending more time with him would only put her at risk of that interest boiling over into actually liking him and the last thing Leilani wanted was to open herself up to getting hurt again. Even the possibility of letting someone close to her heart, to be that vulnerable again, honestly filled her with abject terror.

"Let the man go with you, *keiki*," her father said from where he was helping clean up a nearby table, and Leilani tensed. Jeez, they were really on snooping patrol today. "Show our guest the gym."

She glanced over at her father and gave him a look. Her dad just shook his head and moved on to another section of tables to clean. They thought she was being ridiculous and maybe she was, but she needed to do things on her terms. Stay in control. Control was everything these days.

Holden chuckled and gulped more coffee. "Kiki?"

"Keiki," she corrected him. "It means child in Hawaiian."

Ever since they'd adopted her, the Kims had always called her that. First, because that's what she'd been. A scared fourteen-year-old kid with an uncertain future. Now it was more of a pet name than anything.

Leilani exhaled slowly before pushing to her feet again, her good manners too ingrained to refuse. "Fine. If you want to come with me, you can. Get changed and meet me in the lobby in fifteen minutes. Don't be late, Dr. Ross."

Holden's smile widened, his grateful tone chasing her from the restaurant. "Wouldn't dream of it, Dr. Kim."

The workout facilities at Malu Huna were much like the rest of the resort—clean, spacious and well-appointed— even if the decor was a bit much for his Midwestern sensibilities. More golden palm trees decorated the tile floor here and large murals of the famous Hawaiian sunsets bedecked the walls. There were neat rows of treadmills and stair-climbers, weight machines, stationary bikes and even a boxing area, complete with punching bags and thick mats on the floor.

Holden followed Leilani as she headed for those workout mats, her snug workout clothes clinging to her curves in all the right places. Not that he noticed. He was here to release some tension, not to ogle his colleague. No matter how pretty she was. It had been too long since he'd been with a woman, that was all. The slip of paper with the phone number the waitress had given him flashed in his mind. He hadn't lied to Leilani earlier, but he hadn't been entirely truthful either. He had spoken to the waitress a few days prior about her sick kid and offered to see him, but then the waitress had also asked him out. At the time, he'd declined because he'd been tired and busy and not up for company. But now, with loneliness gnawing at his gut again, maybe he should give the server's invitation second thoughts.

Leilani strapped on a pair of boxing gloves, then turned to face him once more.

Holden stopped short. "Are you going to hit me?"

"Not unless you provoke me." She raised a dark brow at him.

He snorted. "Remind me not to get on your bad side."

"Don't worry. I will." She grinned, then turned to face the heavy bag. "Well, this is the gym. Enjoy your workout."

Looking around, he considered his options. Treadmill was out, with his leg. So were the stair-climbers as they put too much pressure on his still-healing muscles. Stationary bike it was then. He hobbled over and climbed onto one, setting his course to the most difficult one, and began to pedal. Soon his heart was pumping fast, and sweat slicked his face and chest, and he felt the glorious rush of endorphins that always came with a hard work-out. Near the end of his course, Holden glanced over to where he'd left Leilani on the mats and found her working through what looked like kickboxing moves with the punching bag.

Her long hair was piled up in a messy bun atop her head now and her face was flushed from exertion. Her toned arms and back glistened with perspiration beneath the overhead lights as she walloped the heavy bag over and over again. Jab, hook, cross, uppercut. Sweep, cross, kick. Jab, cross, slip. Front kick, back kick. Roundhouse kick. Repeat. Holden found himself entranced.

Once his bike program was done, he moved back over to where she was still dancing around the bag, her movements as coordinated and graceful as any prima ballerina. Even the hot pink boxing gloves didn't detract from Leilani's powerful stance. She looked ready to kick butt and take names. On second thought, just forget the names.

His gaze followed her fists driving hard into the bag. Then he couldn't help continuing to track down her torso to her waist and hips landing finally on her taut butt in those black leggings.

Whoa, boy.

Yep. Dr. Leilani Kim wasn't just pretty. She was gorgeous, no doubt about that. He glanced back up to find her staring at him, her expression flat.

Oops. Busted.

"You know how to fight," he said, for lack of anything better.

She steadied the swinging bag, then punched one glove into the other, blinking at him. "I do. Very well.

Years of training, remember? I'm not afraid to use those skills either."

"I remember you taking down that patient. Don't worry. Point taken." Holden stepped back and chuckled. Back before the shooting he'd been into boxing himself, but he hadn't tried since his injury. He turned to head back to his bike but stopped at the sound of her voice.

"You box?"

"I used to," Holden said, looking back at her over his shoulder. He gestured to his right leg. "Haven't since this though."

"Want to give it a try now?" she asked, tapping the tips of her gloves together. "Be my sparring partner?" Her gaze dipped to his cane then back to his eyes. "I'll take it easy on you."

Whether or not she'd meant that as a challenge didn't matter. He took it as one. The pair of black boxing gloves she tossed in his direction helped too. He caught them one-handed, then narrowed his gaze on her. For the first time in a long time, he wanted to take a chance and burn off a little steam. "Fine."

He strapped on the gloves, then moved back over, setting his cane aside before climbing atop the mat to stand beside Leilani.

"We can stick to bag work, if it's easier on your leg."

"Sparring's fine." He finished closing the Velcro straps around his wrists, then punched his fists together. "Unless you're scared to face off against me?" His tone was teasing. It felt easy to tease her. He didn't want to think about why.

Leilani snorted. "Right. You think you can take me?"

"I think you talk big, but you look pretty small."

"Them's fighting words, mister." She moved several

feet away and faced him before bending her knees and holding her gloves up in front of her face. "All right, Dr. Ross. Show me what you got."

Holden smiled, a genuine one this time, enjoying himself more than he had in a long, long time. "My pleasure, Dr. Kim."

They moved in a small circle on the mat, dodging each other and assessing their opponent. Then, fast as lightning, Leilani struck, landing a solid punch to his chest. He gave her a stunned look and she laughed. "Figured you already had a split lip. Didn't want to damage that handsome face of yours any further."

That stopped him in his tracks.

She thinks I'm handsome?

The reality of her words must've struck Leilani too because the flush in her cheeks grew and she looked away from him. "I mean, I'm taking pity on you. That's all."

Pity. If there was one word sure to set Holden off, it was that one.

All thought of keeping away from Leilani Kim went out the window as he went in for the attack. Apparently still distracted by what she'd said, she didn't react fast enough when he charged toward her and swept his good leg out to knock her feet from under her. Of course, the movement unbalanced him as well, and before Holden knew it, they were both flat on the mat, panting as they tried to catch their breaths in a tangle of limbs.

He managed to recover first, rising on one arm to lean over her. "I don't need your pity, Dr. Kim."

She blinked up at him a moment, then gave a curt nod. "Understood."

"Good." He pushed away to remove one of his gloves

and rake a hand through his sweat-damp hair. "Are you all right?"

"Other than my pride, yes." She sat up next to him and removed her gloves too, several strands of her long, dark hair loose now and curling around her flushed face. "I didn't mean to insult you with what I said, by the way. It was just trash-talking."

"I know." He released a pent-up breath, then wiped off his forehead with the edge of his gray Ohana Medical T-shirt. "The whole pity thing is still a touchy subject for me though, with my leg and all."

"Sorry. I should've realized." She got up and walked over to a small fridge against the wall to pull out two bottles of water, then returned to hand him one. Leilani sat back down on the mat and cracked open her water. "What exactly happened, if you don't mind me asking?"

He gulped down half his bottle of water before answering, hoping to wash away the lump of anxiety that still rose every time someone asked about his injury. He did mind, usually, but today felt different. Maybe because they were the only ones in the gym, and that lent a certain air of intimacy. Through the windows across the room, he could see a bit of the gloom outside had lifted and weak rays of sunshine beamed in. Maybe it was time to let some of his past out of the bag, at least a little. He shrugged and fiddled with his gloves once more. "I got shot. Shattered my femur."

"Yikes. That's awful." Leilani grabbed the white towel she'd tossed on the floor nearby when they'd first arrived and wiped off her face. He glanced sideways at her and did his best not to notice the small bead of sweat tickling down the side of her throat. Tried to stop the sudden thought of how salty that might taste, how warm her skin might be against his tongue.

Wait. What?

He looked away fast as she wrapped the towel around her neck, then faced him once more.

"So," she said, her clear tone cutting through the roar of blood pounding in his ears, not from anxiety this time, but from unexpected, unwanted lust. "Is that when you took the bullet to your shoulder as well?"

Holden nodded, not trusting his voice at present, then drank more water. He didn't want Leilani Kim. Not that way. She was his coworker. She was just being nice. She was drinking her water too, drawing his attention to the sleek muscles of her throat as they worked, the pound of the pulse point at the base of her neck, the curve of her breasts in that tight sports bra.

Oh God.

Move. He needed to move. He started to get to his feet, but Leilani stopped him with a hand on his arm. "I'm sorry that happened to you. I know what it's like to be in a situation where you feel helpless and alone."

The hint of pain in her tone stunned him into staying put. From what he could see, she'd had a fairy-tale life here in paradise, raised in this wedding cake of a hotel.

"How's that? And please, call me Holden," he said, more curious than ever about this enigmatic, beautiful woman. To try to lighten the mood, he cracked a joke. "You get hit by a pineapple on the way to surf the waves?"

Her small smile fell and it felt like the brightening room darkened. She shook her head and looked away. "No. More like hit by a truck and spent six months in the hospital."

"Oh." For a second, Holden just took that in, unsure what else to say. Of course, his analytical mind wanted to know more, demanded details, but he didn't feel comfortable enough to do so. Finally, he managed, "I had no idea."

"No. Most people don't." She sighed and rolled her neck, reaching back to rub her nape again, same as she had the other day in the ER with that combative patient. Then she stood and started gathering her things. "Well, I should go get ready for work."

Of all people, Holden knew a retreat when he saw one. He got up as well, reaching for his cane to take the weight off his now-aching leg. Doing that foot sweep on Leilani hadn't been the most genius move ever, even if his whole side now tingled from the feel of her body briefly pressed to his.

He grabbed his water bottle and limped after her toward the exit, pausing to hold the door for her. Before walking out himself, he looked over toward the windows across the gym one last time. "Hey, the sun's out again."

Leilani glanced in the same direction, then gave him a tiny grin. "Funny how that works, huh? Wait long enough and it always comes back out. See you around, Holden."

"Bye, Dr. Kim," he said, watching her walk away, then stop at the end of the hall and turn back to him.

"Leilani," she called. "Anyone who leg-sweeps me gets to be on a first-name basis."

CHAPTER FOUR

THE ER AT Ohana Medical Center was hopping the following Wednesday and Leilani was in her element. She was halfway through a twelve-hour shift, and so far she'd dealt with four broken limbs, one case of appendicitis that she'd passed on to a gastro surgeon for removal, and two box jellyfish stings that had required treatment beyond the normal vinegar rinse and ice. The full moon was Friday and that's when the jellyfish population tended to increase near the beaches to mate. There weren't any official warnings posted yet, according to the patient's husband, but that didn't mean there weren't jellyfish present. They were a year-round hazard in Hawaii.

So yeah, a typical day in the neighborhood.

Leilani liked being busy though. That's what made emergency medicine such a good fit for her. Kept her out of trouble, as her parents always said.

Trouble like thinking about that gym encounter with Holden Ross the week prior.

She suppressed a shiver that ran through her at the memory of his hard body pressed against hers on that mat, the heat of him going through her like a bolt of lightning, making her imagine things that were completely off-limits as far as her colleague was concerned.

Since that day, they'd passed each other a few times in the halls, both at the hospital and at the hotel, but hadn't really said more than a friendly greeting. Just as well, since time hadn't seemed to lessen the tingling that passed through her nerve endings whenever he was near. In fact, if anything, the fact they'd taken a tumble on that mat together only seemed to intensify her awareness of him. Which probably explained why she was still hung up on the whole thing. Leilani tried never to let her guard down but Holden had somehow managed to get around her usual barriers.

Boundaries were key to her maintaining control. And control required no distractions.

Distractions led to accidents and accidents led to…

Shaking off the unwanted stab of sorrow in her heart, she concentrated on the notes she was currently typing into her tablet computer at the nurses' station. The EMTs had just radioed in with another patient headed their way and she wanted to get caught up as much as possible before taking on another case.

As she documented her treatment for the latest jellyfish sting patient—visible tentacles removed from sting site, antihistamine for mild allergic reaction, hydrocortisone cream for itching and swelling, ice packs as needed—she half listened to the commotion around her for news of the EMTs arrival with her next patient. She'd just closed out the file she'd been working on when the voice of the sister of one of her earlier patients, a guy who'd broken his arm while hiking near the Diamond Head Crater, broke through her thoughts.

"Doctor?" the woman said, coming down the hall. "I need to ask you something."

Leilani glanced over, ready to answer whatever questions the woman had, then stopped short as the woman headed straight past her and made a beeline for Holden, who'd just come out of an exam room.

He glanced up at the buxom blonde and blinked several times. "How can I help you, ma'am?"

"My brother was in here earlier and I'm concerned he won't take the prescription they gave him correctly, even after the other doctor explained it to him. She was Hawaiian, I think, and—"

"Dr. Kim is the head of Emergency Medicine. I'm sure the instructions she gave him were clear." Holden searched the area and locked eyes with Leilani. "But if you still have concerns, let's go see if she has a few moments to talk to you again, Mrs....?"

"Darla," the woman said, batting her eyelashes and grinning wide.

Leilani bit back a snicker at her flagrant flirting.

"And it's Miss. I'm single. Besides, I'm old-fashioned and prefer a male doctor."

Holden's expression shifted from confused to cornered in about two seconds flat. Darla didn't want medical advice. She wanted a date. Leilani would've laughed out loud at his obvious discomfort if there wasn't a strange niggle eating into her core. Not jealousy because that would be stupid. She had no reason to care if anybody flirted with Holden. It was none of her business. And it wasn't like men hadn't tried to flirt with Leilani in the ER either. It was another occupational hazard. No, what should have bothered her more was the woman doubting her medical expertise. Shoulders squared, she raised a brow and waited for their approach.

Holden cleared his throat and stepped around Darla to head to the nurses' station and Leilani. "Dr. Kim is one of the best physicians I've worked with. She's the person to advise you and your brother on his medications, as she's familiar with his case." He stopped beside Leilani at the desk, tiny dots of crimson staining his high cheekbones. "Dr. Kim, this lady has more questions about her brother's prescription."

Leilani gave him a curt nod, then proceeded to go over the same information she'd given to Darla's brother an hour prior. Steroids weren't exactly rocket science, and from the way the woman continued to focus on Holden's backside and not Leilani, it seemed Darla could have cared less anyway. Finally, Darla went on her way and Leilani exhaled slowly as the EMTs radioed in their ETA of one minute.

Showtime.

Refocusing quickly, she grabbed a fresh gown and mask from the rack nearby and suited up, aware of Holden's gaze on her as she did so. Her skin prickled under the weight of his stare, but she shook it off. The incoming patient needed her undivided attention, not Dr. Ross.

"What's the new case?" Holden asked, handing his tablet back to the nurse behind the desk. "Need help?"

"Maybe," Leilani said, tying the mask around her neck. "Stick close by just in case."

"Will do." He took a gown and mask for himself, then followed her down the hall to the automatic doors leading in from the ambulance bay. His presence beside her felt oddly reassuring, which only rattled her more. She was used to handling things on her own. Safe, secure, solo. That's how she liked it.

Isn't it?

Too late to stew about it now. The doors swished open and the EMTs rushed in with a young man on a gurney. Leilani raced down the hall next to the patient as the EMT in charge gave her a rundown.

"Eighteen-year-old male surfer struck in the neck by his surfboard," the paramedic said. "Difficulty breathing that's worsened over time."

They raced into trauma bay two and Leilani moved in to examine the patient, who was gasping like a fish out of water. "Sir, can you speak? Does it feel like your throat is closing?"

The kid nodded, his eyes wide with panic.

"Okay," Leilani said, keeping her voice calm. "Is it hard to breathe right now?"

The patient nodded again.

"Are you nodding because it hurts to talk or because you can't?" Holden asked, moving in on the other side of the bed once the EMTs got the patient moved from the gurney.

"I…" the kid rasped. "C-can't."

"No intubation, then," Holden said, holding up a hand to stop the nurse with the tracheal tube. "Dr. Kim, would you like me to consult?"

Nice. The other trauma surgeons on staff usually just commandeered a case, rarely asking for Leilani's permission to intercede. Having Holden do so now was refreshing, especially since she'd asked him to stick close by earlier. It showed a level of professional respect that she liked a lot. Plus, it would give her a chance to see firsthand how he handled himself with patients. For weeks now, the nurses had been praising his bedside manner and coolness under pressure. About time Leilani got to see what she was up against if they were both vying for the directorship.

"Yes, please, Dr. Ross." She grabbed an oxygen tube to insert into the kid's nose to help his respiration. "Okay, sir. Breathe in through your nose. Good. One more time."

The kid gasped again. "I c-can't."

Leilani placed her hand on his shoulder. "You're doing fine. I know it hurts."

Holden finished his exam then stepped back to speak to relay orders to the nurse taking the patient's vitals. "We need a CTA of his neck and X-rays, please. Depending on what those show, I may need to do a fiber-optic thoracoscopy. Call ENT for a consult as well, please."

"Where's my son?" a man's voice shouted from out in the hall. "Please let me see him!"

After signing off on the orders, Holden moved aside to let the techs roll the patient out of the trauma room, then grabbed Leilani to go speak to the father. "Sir, your son was injured while surfing," Holden said, after pulling down his mask. "He's getting the best care possible between myself and Dr. Kim. Can you tell me your son's name?"

"Tommy," the man said. "Tommy Schrader. I'm his father, Bill Schrader."

"Thank you, Mr. Schrader." Leilani led the man down the hall to a private waiting room while Holden headed off with the team to complete the tests on the patient. "Let's have a seat in here."

"Will my boy be all right?" Mr. Schrader asked. "What's happened to him?"

"From what the EMTs said when they brought your son in, Tommy was surfing and was struck in the throat by his surfboard. He's got some swelling in his neck and is having trouble breathing." It was obvious the man cared deeply for his son and it was always hard to give difficult news to loved ones. In her case, they'd had to sedate her after delivering the news about her family's deaths. At least Tommy was still alive and getting the treatment he needed.

"When I got the call from the police, I panicked. I told Tommy the surf was too rough today, but he didn't listen." Mr. Schrader scrubbed his hand over his haggard face. "All kinds of crazy things went through my mind. I've never been so scared in all my life."

"Completely understandable, Mr. Schrader. But please know we're doing all we can, and we'll keep you updated on his progress as soon as we know more. They're doing X-rays and a CT scan on him now to determine the extent of damage and the next steps for treatment." She patted the man's shoulder, then stood. "Can I get you anything to drink?"

"No, no. I'm good. I just want to know my son will be okay."

"He's in the best hands possible," Leilani said. "Let me go check on his status again and I'll be right back."

"Thank you," Mr. Schrader said. "I'm sorry I don't know your name."

"Dr. Kim." She gave him a kind smile. "Just sit tight and I'll be back in as soon as we know more."

"Thank you, Dr. Kim," Mr. Schrader said.

Leilani left him and headed up to radiology to check in with Holden. She'd no more than stepped off the elevators when he waved her over to look at the films.

"See how narrow this is?" Holden asked her, pointing at the films of the kid's trachea. "There's definite swelling in his airway. In fact, given that there's maybe only one or two millimeters open at most, it's starting to close off completely. There should be a finger's width all the way up."

Definitely not good, especially since the airway normally narrowed at that point anyway, right before the vocal cords. Which brought up the next issues.

"What about his voice box?" she asked.

"That's my concern," Holden said, the grayish light from the X-ray viewer casting deep shadows on the hollows of his cheeks and under his eyes. "Looks like the surfboard made a direct hit on that area. The voice box could've been broken from the impact. It's a high-risk injury in a high-risk area of the body." He shook his head and leaned in closer to the films. "At least this explains his trouble breathing."

"Are you going to operate?" Leilani asked.

Holden exhaled slowly. "No, not yet. Hate to do that to a kid so young. My advice would be to treat him with steroids first and see if the swelling goes down. Watch him like a hawk though. If conservative treatment doesn't work, then I'll go in with the thoracoscopy."

"Agreed." Leilani stepped back and smiled. Working with Holden felt natural, comfortable. Like they were a team. "Best to keep him in the ER then for the time being. That way if he needs emergency assistance, we're there."

"Yep. Let's do it."

She and Holden rode back down to the trauma bay with the medical team and Tommy, then called his father into the room.

Holden and Leilani exchanged looks, then she nodded. He stepped forward to take the lead. "Mr. Schrader, I'm sorry to tell you this is a very, very serious situation. Your son's airway is currently compromised due to swelling from the surfboard strike. It's possible his voice box had been damaged. If that's the case, it could have long-term effects on his speech."

"Oh God." Mr. Schrader moved in beside his son and took the kid's hand. "I told you not to go surfing today. I was so worried."

"I know," Tommy managed to croak out, clinging to his dad's hand. "Sorry."

"Our biggest concern though, at this point," Holden continued, "is that if his larynx—his voice box—is too badly damaged, your son runs the risk of losing his ability to breathe. We need to keep him here at the hospital, in the ER, for at least the next twelve hours for observation. That way if his condition worsens, we can rush him into surgery immediately, if needed. I'd also like to get a consult from one of the throat specialists on staff to get their opinion."

"Whatever you need to do," Mr. Schrader said. "I just want my son to be okay."

"Great. Thank you." Holden stepped back and glanced at Leilani again. "Both Dr. Kim and I will check on Tommy periodically through the night to keep an eye on him then."

"Yes, we will. You won't be alone." Leilani leaned in to place the call button in the kid's hand and give him a reassuring smile. Once upon a time, that had been her in a hospital bed—scared and unsure about the future. "And if you feel your breathing gets worse at any point, you just press that button and we'll rush back in right away, okay?"

Tommy gave a hesitant nod.

"Someone will always be here for you, Tommy," Holden said, meeting Leilani's gaze. "I promise. We're not going to let anything else happen to you."

The kid swallowed, then winced.

"Don't worry. We'll be in here checking on you so often you'll get sick of seeing us." Leilani winked, then headed toward the door with Holden. "Promise."

"And I'll be here too, son," his dad said, pulling up a chair to the beside.

She and Holden walked back to the nurses' station, discarding their masks and gowns in the biohazard bin and stopping to wash their hands at the sink nearby. His limp seemed less pronounced today, though he still used his cane to take the weight off his right leg.

She glanced over at him and smiled as she soaped up, then rinsed off. "You handled that case well."

"Thanks." He smiled, then winced, tossing his used paper towels in the trash and reaching up to touch the sutures in his lower lip.

"Stitches bothering you?" she asked, leaning a bit closer to inspect his wound. "Looks like it's healing well."

"I'm fine. It just stings a bit when I forget it's there," he said, holding up a tube of lip balm. "This helps though."

"Glad to hear it." Leilani turned away from the cherry flavored lip balm he held up. That was her favorite flavor. And now, for some reason, her mind kept wondering what his kisses would taste like with cherries in the mix. Ugh. Not good. Not good at all. She stepped back and looked anywhere but at him. "So, I should probably get back to work on another case then."

"Yeah, me too." He fiddled with the head of his cane, frowning slightly. "Hey, um, I meant to ask you about the luau."

"Luau?" she repeated, like she was channeling her pet parrot. Her pulse kicked up a notch. Damn. She'd been hoping he'd forget about all that. Apparently not. She forced a smile she didn't quite feel and flexed her fingers to relax them. Considering she'd just been having inappropriate thoughts about this man—her coworker— if she was wise, she'd get the heck out of there as soon as possible. Unfortunately, her feet seemed to have other ideas, because they stayed firmly planted where she was.

At least he seemed as awkward as she felt about it all, shuffling his feet and fumbling over his words. It was actually quite endearing... Leilani's heart pinched a little at the sweetness, before she stopped herself.

Keep it professional, girl.

"The other day, last week, uh," he said, keeping his gaze lowered like he was a nervous schoolkid and not a highly successful surgeon. "Anyway, I think your dad mentioned the luau at the hotel and I'd seen some flyers on it too, and I wondered if you still wanted to take me." He hazarded a glance up and caught her eye. "Not that I'll hold you to that. I just..." He exhaled slowly and ran his free hand through his hair, leaving the dark curls in adorable disarray.

No. Not adorable. No, no, no.

But even as she thought that, the simmering awareness bubbling inside her boiled over into blatant interest without her consent. Damn. This was beyond inconvenient. Of all the men for her to be interested in now, it had to be Holden Ross.

He huffed out a breath, then cursed quietly before straightening and meeting her gaze head-on as his words tumbled out in a rush. "Look. I don't get out much and I'd like to see some sights while I'm here, and since you offered the other day, I thought I'd take you up on that, if the offer…if it still stands. Not a date, because I don't do that. Just as two people, colleagues…" He hung his head. "I'm off tomorrow and Friday."

Leilani blinked at him a moment, stunned. Blood thundered in her ears and she turned away to grab her tablet from behind the desk, needing something, anything, to keep herself busy, to keep herself from agreeing to his invitation and more. Because for some crazy reason that's exactly what she wanted to do.

Think, girl. Think.

Saying yes could lead to a friendship between them beyond work, could lead to those uncomfortable tingles of like for this guy going a whole lot further into other *l* words. Not *love*, because that was off the table, but another one with a capital *L. Lust.* Because yeah, Holden really was just her type. Tall, dark, gorgeous. Smart, funny, sexy as all get out.

So, she should definitely say no. He was her coworker, her potential rival.

Except that would be rude. And she just couldn't bring herself to be rude to him. Maybe it was that haunted look in her eyes she spied sometimes. Maybe it was his obvious awkwardness around commitment.

I don't date.

Well, neither did she at present. Or maybe it was the

air of brokenness about him that called to the same old wounded parts in her.

Whatever it was, she didn't want to turn him down, even though she should.

There was one problem though.

She looked back at him over her shoulder as she brought up the next patient's information on her screen. "Malu Huna's luaus are only on Friday nights. And I have to work tomorrow. If you wanted to see the sights on Friday," she said, taking a deep breath to calm her racing nerves, "then I guess we could. It will make for a long day though. Are you sure you're up to that?"

"I am if you are," he said, his cane clinking against the desk as he moved closer. "I'll double up on my pain pills so I'm ready for anything."

Ready for anything.

Damn if those words, spoken in that deep velvet voice of his, didn't conjure a whole new batch of inappropriate thoughts. The two of them on the beach, holding hands and running into the waves together, lying in the sand afterward, making out like two horny teens, the feel of that dark stubble on his jaw scraping her cheeks, her neck, her chest, lower still…

Oh boy. I'm in trouble here.

Heat stormed her cheeks and she swiveled to face him, not realizing how close they were until it was too late. Her hand brushed his solid, warm chest before she snatched it away. Holden's hazel eyes flared with the same awareness jolting through her, before he quickly hid it behind a frown.

"Look, if you don't want to—"

"No, it's fine. I promised you and I always keep my word." She focused on the file on her screen again, trying in vain to calm her whirling thoughts. This was so not like her. She never went gaga over men. Yet here she was, blushing and stammering and acting like an idiot over the last man on Earth she should be attracted to. And yet, she was. Much as she hated to admit it.

Gah! Images of them lying together on that mat in the hotel gym zoomed back fast and furious to her mind. No. If she was going to get through this with her sanity and her heart intact, she needed to think logically about it. She'd show him her island home, not just the tourist sights, but her favorite spots too. Besides, it might give her a chance to find out more about his relationship with Dr. King and his real motives for being here in Hawaii. Taken in that light, she'd be a fool not to take him up on his offer, right? She took a deep breath, then set her tablet aside. "Fine. We'll tour the town, then end with the luau. Meet me in the lobby at the hotel at 8:00 a.m. the day after tomorrow and don't be late."

Holden opened his mouth, closed it, then he smiled— the slow little one that made her toes curl in her comfy white running shoes. Ugh. No more of that. She turned away to head into her next exam room as his surprised tone revealed an equal amount of shock on his part. "Uh…okay. Eight o'clock on Friday it is."

Four hours later, Holden was finishing up his shift by checking for the last time with Tommy Schrader. The kid was lucky. The steroids had helped reduce the swelling in his larynx and it didn't look like the thoracoscopy would be necessary after all.

When Holden arrived upstairs to Tommy's room, several of the kid's surfer friends were there, along with Tommy's father. Tommy was holding court like a king on his throne from his hospital bed, sun-streaked shaggy blond hair hanging in his face and his voice like gravel in a blender. But the fact the kid was speaking at all was a minor miracle. His injury could've been so much worse, and Holden was glad such a young guy wouldn't carry lifelong scars from his accident.

Unlike Holden himself.

He cleared his throat at the door to the hospital room to announce his presence. "Sorry if this is a bad time. Just wanted to check in on my patient one more time before my shift is over." He limped into the room with his cane and smiled at Mr. Schrader and the new guests. "Tommy's very lucky."

"Dudes, you have no idea," Tommy rasped out, smiling at Holden, then his friends. "They were gonna stick a camera up my nose and down my throat and everything."

"Whoa," his friends said, both as shaggy and sunburned as Tommy. "Man, that's gnarly. You were gonna be awake for that?"

"Patients are usually awake for thoracoscopy, yes," Holden confirmed as he reached Tommy's beside and leaned closer to examine the kid's throat. The swelling was greatly reduced, even from the last time Holden had checked him about an hour prior. He'd be fine to discharge.

He straightened and turned to Mr. Schrader, who was sitting on a chair near the window. "Your son appears to be healing just fine now, though Dr. Kim will continue to check on him for the remainder of his stay. I don't imagine there'll be any lingering effects, but I'll leave orders to discharge him with another round of steroids and some anti-inflammatory meds too. Then have him check in with your family physician in two weeks."

"Sounds good." The father shook Holden's hand. "Thanks so much, Doc. Now that I know my son's gonna be all right, once I get him home I'll make sure his older brothers keep an eye on him too. And try to talk him out of surfing so close to a full moon again."

Holden grinned and turned back to Tommy. "Listen to your dad. Take care, Tommy."

"Thanks, Doc. *Mahalo*," the kid said, shaking Holden's hand too. "I'll be sure to thank the pretty lady doc too. You guys make a good team. She your girlfriend?"

"Son," Mr. Schrader said, his voice rife with warning. "Don't mind him, Dr. Ross. That's all him and his friends think about these days when they're not surfing. Girls."

"I'll pass along gratitude to Dr. Kim," Holden said, dodging the uncomfortable questions and ignoring the squeeze of anxiety in his chest it caused. "Take care, all."

"*Mahalo*, Doc!" Tommy called again as Holden walked from the room to the nurses' station down the hall.

He should feel relieved to have another successful patient outcome under his belt, but now all he could think about was Leilani and their upcoming date on Friday.

Wait. Scratch that. Not a date.

He hadn't lied when he'd told her he didn't do that. Life was too unpredictable for long-term commitments. The shooting had taught him that. Nothing was permanent, especially love. So now he chose short, sweet, no strings attached affairs. No deeper, messy, scary emotions involved, thanks. No connections beyond the physical. No chance to have his heart ripped out and shredded to pieces. Because that's what he wanted.

Isn't it?

Not that it mattered. He and Leilani Kim were work colleagues, nothing more. Best to keep his head down and focus on his work, then move on when this stint ended. That was the safest bet. And Holden was all about safety these days.

She'd show him around the city, then take him to the luau at the resort, as promised. That's all. Nothing more. And sure, he couldn't stop thinking about the feel of her beneath him on that stupid gym mat, the sweet jasmine and lemon scent of her hair, the warm brush of her skin against his and...

Oh God.

He was such an idiot. What the hell had he been thinking to bring up her invitation to the luau? He hadn't been thinking, that was the problem. Or more to the point, he'd been thinking with his libido and not his brain. Memories of her dressed in those formfitting leggings and tank top at the gym that day, how she might wrap those shapely legs of hers around him instead, and hold him close, kiss him, run her fingers through his hair. He shuddered.

No. No, no, no.

With more effort than should be necessary to concentrate, Holden finished electronically signing off on his notes on the Tommy Schrader case, then left instructions for his discharge for Leilani before handing it all over to the nurse waiting behind the desk.

"Dr. King asked to see you upstairs in her office when you have a moment, Dr. Ross," the nurse said.

"Thanks." Probably about that project she'd mentioned to him before. He took a deep breath, then headed for the elevators. The clock on the wall said it was nearly time for him to leave. Good. He'd see Helen, then head back to the ER to hand off his cases to the next physician on duty before going back to the hotel for some much-needed sleep.

Besides, talking to Helen should be a good distraction from his unwanted thoughts about Leilani. The elevator dinged and he stepped on board then pushed the button for the fifth floor, where the administrative offices were located.

He had to get his head on straight again before Friday. Hell, if he was really serious about keeping to himself, he'd cancel the whole day altogether. Given the surprised look on her face when she'd offered to show him around, she'd probably be glad to be rid of him as well. But then if he did cancel, she might take it the wrong way, and the last thing he wanted was to offend her. They still had to work together, after all.

You guys make a good team.

Tommy's words from earlier echoed through his head. The worst part was, they were true.

Working with Leilani on that case had felt seamless, effortless, *right.*

Which was just wrong, in Holden's estimation.

He didn't want partnerships anymore, professionally or personally. Getting too close to people only made you vulnerable and weak, especially when they could be taken from you so easily.

Ding!

The elevator doors swished open and Holden stepped out into the lobby on the administrative floor. Thick carpet padded his footsteps as he headed over to the receptionist's desk in the middle of the plush leather-and-glass sitting area.

"Hi. Holden Ross to see Helen King, please," he said,

feeling out of place and underdressed in his shift-old scrubs and sneakers.

"Dr. King's been expecting you, Dr. Ross." She pointed down a hallway to her left. "Last door on the right."

"Thanks." He gave the woman a polite smile, then headed for the office she'd indicated. The other times he'd met with Helen here in Hawaii, it had been outside the hospital, either at her home near Waikiki or at the fancy restaurant she'd taken him to on his first night in the city. Other than that, he'd never been up here, since regular old human resources was in another building entirely, half a block down from the medical center. He made his way to the end of the hall and stopped to admire the amazing view from the floor-to-ceiling glass wall beside the office before knocking on the dark wood door.

"Come in," Helen called from inside, and Holden entered the office.

For a moment, he took in the understated elegance of the place. It was Helen to a T, no-nonsense yet comfortable. "Wow, this is a big step up from Chicago, huh?"

Helen chuckled, her husky voice helping to soothe his earlier anxiety. "It doesn't suck. Please come in, Holden. Have a seat."

He did so, in a large wingback leather chair in front of her desk that probably cost more than his rent back home. As always, Helen's desk was spotless, with stacks of files neatly placed in bins and every pen just so. "The nurse downstairs said you wanted to see me?"

"I wanted to see how you're settling in," she said, sitting back in her black leather executive chair that dwarfed her petite frame. With her short white hair and sparkling blue eyes, she'd always reminded Holden of a certain British actress of a certain age, who took no crap from anyone. "We haven't talked in a few weeks. How are you liking things here at Ohana?"

"Fine." He did his best to relax but found it difficult. He and Helen had been friends long enough for him to suspect this wasn't just a social call. They could've gone to the pub for that. "The facilities are top-notch and the staff is great."

Better than great, his mind chimed in as he recalled Leilani.

Not that he'd mention his unwanted attraction to his coworker to Helen. The woman had been trying to get him married off since they'd worked together back in Chicago. If she even suspected a hint of chemistry between him and Leilani, she'd be all over it worse than the Spanish Inquisition.

"Glad to hear you like it." Helen steepled her fingers, then watched him over the top of them, her gaze narrowed, like M getting ready to assign her best secret agent a new kill. "But do you like it enough to consider staying?"

"What?" Holden tore his gaze away from the stunning views of the ocean in the distance and focused on Helen once more, his chest tightening. He frowned. "No. I'm locum tenens."

"I know," she said, sitting forward to rest her arms atop her desk. "But what if you weren't."

The low-grade anxiety constantly swirling in his chest rose higher, constricting his vocal cords. "But I am. You know I don't want to get tied down to anywhere. Not yet."

Maybe not ever again.

Helen blinked at him several times before exhaling slowly, her expression morphing from confident to concerned. "I'm worried about you, Holden. You've been on your own since the shooting, jetting off to a new place every few months, no connections, no home."

"I'm fine," he said, forcing the words. "Look, I thought you called me here to talk about that project you mentioned, not dissect my personal life."

"Are you fine though?" Her blue gaze narrowed, far too perceptive for his tastes. She sighed and stood, coming around the desk and leaning her hips back against it as she changed the subject. "Well, all that aside... Fine, let's discuss the project then."

Holden released his pent-up breath, his lungs aching for oxygen, and stared at the floor beneath his feet. Helen had saved his life after the shooting. Stitching up his wounds and staunching his blood loss until the orthopedic surgeons could work their magic on his leg and shoulder. Without her, there was a good chance he would've ended up six feet under, just like David.

An unexpected pang of grief stabbed his chest. Even a year later, he still missed his best friend like it was yesterday. The funeral. The awful days afterward, walking around like a zombie, no emotions, no light, no hope.

Still, he was here. He was coming back to life slowly, painfully, whether he wanted to or not. Like a limb that had fallen asleep, pins and needles stabbed him relentlessly as the emotions he'd suppressed for so long returned. Maybe that was why he felt so drawn to Leilani—her vibrant spirit, the sense that perhaps in some weird way she understood what he'd been through, how she made him feel things he'd thought he'd never feel again.

Plus, he owed Helen a debt he could never repay. That's why he was here in Hawaii. Why he was here now. She'd saved his life and his leg. The least he could do was hear her out. He cleared his throat, then asked, "What kind of project is it?"

"Twofold, actually." Helen clasped her hands in front of her. "First, our national accreditation is coming up for renewal next year and we need to make sure all of our security policies are up-to-date for the ER. I'd like you to help with that."

Holden swallowed hard and forced his tense shoulders to relax. "I can do that."

"Good." Helen glanced out the windows then back to him again. "Secondly, you know I'm looking for a new director of emergency medicine, yes?"

"Yes," he said. "But I'm here as a trauma surgeon."

"True. But you've got the experience and the temperament to head a department, Holden." She crossed her arms. "You were on track to run the ER back in Chicago, before the shooting."

He had been. That was true. But those ambitions had died along with David that day. He didn't want to be responsible for all those people, for all those lives. What if he failed again?

"I don't want that anymore. I'm happy with the temporary stint." His response sounded flat to his own ears and his heart pinched slightly despite knowing he couldn't even consider taking on a more permanent role. "Besides, Dr. Kim is doing a great job as temporary director. Why not offer it to her?"

"She's in the running, to be sure," Helen said before pushing away from the desk and walking over to the windows nearby. "But I like to keep my options open.

And it's been nice having you here, Holden. I won't lie. We're friends. I know you. Trust you. Dr. Kim seems more than competent and her record at Ohana is outstanding, but every time I try to get to know her better, she shuts me down. I'm not sure I can work with someone I don't know and trust implicitly."

Holden had noticed Leilani deftly skirting his questions around her past too. Then again, he had no room to talk. He hadn't told her anything about what had happened to him either.

He exhaled slowly and raked a hand through his hair. He didn't like the idea of spying for Helen, no matter how much he owed her. Maybe he should cancel Friday, just so it wouldn't come back to bite him later, one way or another. Shut down any semblance of something more between him and Leilani before it ever really started. The fact he seemed more drawn to her each time they were together scared him more than anything, to be honest, and Holden was no coward. But damn if he wanted to open himself up to a world of hurt again, and some hidden part of him sensed that getting closer to Leilani would bring heartbreak for sure.

"I don't feel comfortable spying for you," he said bluntly. "Not on a colleague."

"No," Helen said, giving him a small smile. "I didn't imagine you would. Well, that's fine. Just keep an eye out during the project. If you see anything you think I should know about, let me know. Oh, and I haven't talked to Dr. Kim about it yet, so keep it under your hat, until I do. Okay?"

"Okay." Seemed an odd request, but an innocent one. "No problem. Anything else?"

"Nope. That's it." Helen walked back around her desk

and took a seat. "I've got work to do, so get out of my office."

He chuckled and stood, his cane sinking into the thick carpet as he leaned his weight on it. "Let me know when it's safe to mention the project to Leilani. I'll be out until the weekend."

Helen gave him a quizzical look at his use of Dr. Kim's first name, and he kicked himself mentally. Then she winked and grinned as he hobbled toward the door.

"Enjoy your days off," she called after him.

"Thanks," he said, gritting his teeth against the soreness in his thigh. He needed to finish up his shift, then get back to the hotel, take a shower, rest, recharge, decide whether to cancel on Friday or spend the day with the one woman who'd somehow gotten under his skin despite all his wishes to the contrary.

"Oh, and Holden?" Helen called when he was halfway into the hall.

"Yeah?" He peeked his head back inside the office.

"Don't stay cooped up your whole time here in Hawaii," she said, as if reading his thoughts. "Get out and live a little. Trust me—you'll be glad you did."

Holden headed back down the hall and over the elevators, unable to shake the sense of fate weighing heavy on his shoulders. Too bad he didn't believe in destiny anymore. One random act of violence had changed all that forever.

Still, as he headed back down to the ER his old friend's words kept running through his head, forcing him to reconsider canceling his Friday plans with Leilani.

Get out and live a little. Trust me—you'll be glad you did...

CHAPTER FIVE

At seven fifty-eight on Friday morning, Leilani stood behind the reception desk at her parents' resort, feeding her parrot, U'i, and wondering if it was too late to fake a stomach bug to get out of her day with Holden.

"Who's a pretty bird?" U'i squawked, followed by a string of curses in three languages—Mandarin, Hawaiian and English.

Leilani snorted and fed him another hunk of fresh pineapple. She'd had him as a pet since right after the accident and loved him with all her heart, even though he acted like a brat and swore like a sailor sometimes. Considering he was sixteen and African grays typically lived as long as humans, U'i was definitely in his terrible teen years.

"More," he screeched when she wasn't fast enough with the next hunk of fruit. He took it in his black beak, then held on to a slice of orange with one foot while cocking his head at her and blinking his dark eyes. "Thanks, baby."

"You're welcome, baby," she said in return, scratching his feathered head with her finger and grinning. "Mama loves you."

"Mama loves you," U'i repeated, before devouring his treat.

"Hey," a deep male voice said from behind her, causing her heart to flip.

Leilani set aside the cup of fruit she'd snagged from the breakfast buffet in the dining room, then wiped her hands on the legs of her denim shorts before turning slowly to face Holden. *Too late to run now*, she supposed. She gave him a smile and prayed she didn't look as nervous as she felt. "Hey."

In truth, she'd spent the last twenty-four hours seriously questioning her sanity for offering to be Holden's tour guide today. Sure, she wanted to get to know him better, but that was a double-edged sword. Getting to know him better risked getting to like him better. And liking him even more than she did now was a definite no-no, considering she melted a little more inside each time she saw him.

Like now, when he was standing there, looking effortlessly gorgeous in a pair of navy board shorts and a yellow Hawaiian shirt that rivaled any of the loud numbers her dad wore. The open V of his collar beckoned her eyes to trail slowly down his tanned chest to his trim hips and strong, sexy, tanned calves. God. How was that even possible? Their schedules at the hospital were nuts. Who had time to soak up the sunshine? Apparently, Holden did, since he looked like he'd walked straight off a "hot hunks in paradise" poster.

He shuffled his feet and switched his cane from one side to the other, making her realize she'd been staring. Self-conscious now, she turned back to her pet and fed him another chunk of pineapple from the cup.

"Who's your friend?" Holden asked.

"This is U'i," she said, leaning in to kiss the bird's head.

"Huey?" Holden asked, stepping closer to look at the parrot, who was eyeballing him back.

"No. *U'i*," Leilani corrected him. "No *h*. It means *handsome* in Hawaiian."

"Ah." He reached up toward the bird, then hesitated. "Does he bite?"

"Only if he doesn't like you." She snorted at Holden's startled expression, then took pity on him, holding out the fruit cup toward him. "Here, feed him some of this. U'i's never met food he didn't like."

Sure enough, her traitorous pet snagged the hunk of melon from Holden's fingers, then gave him an infatuated coo that Leilani was lucky to hear even after a half hour of cuddles and tummy rubs. Seemed Holden's considerable charms worked on more than just her.

"African gray, right?" Holden asked, bravely stroking a finger over U'i's head.

"Correct." Leilani smiled despite herself. "You a bird fan?"

"A friend of mine back in med school had one. Smart as a whip and snarky too."

"Yep, that's my guy here." She gave her beloved pet one more kiss, then stepped away fast. Holden moved as well, causing his arm to brush hers, sending tingles of awareness through her already overtaxed nervous system. "So, are you, uh, ready to go?"

"Whenever you are," Holden said, stepping back and giving her a too-bright smile. "Doubled my pain meds, so lead onward."

For the second time since their conversation in the ER

on Wednesday, the thought popped into her head that maybe he was as nervous about all this as she was. After all, he'd been stammering and shifting around as much as her, his frown still fresh in her mind. She'd assumed it was because he didn't really want to spend time with her, but now she wondered if it went deeper than that.

"Did you get Tommy Schrader released okay—the surfboard patient? He was doing much better the last time I checked. He told me *mahalo*."

"Yep. He was doing much better when I discharged him. Gave him your scripts too. I'm glad there wasn't any permanent damage to his voice box." She wiped her hands off again and tossed away the empty fruit cup before walking back around the desk and beckoning for Holden to follow her. Well, regardless of how he felt about things, they were both stuck together for the day now. Correction, day and evening, since they had the luau tonight after their day of sightseeing. Then they could go back to their separate lives. Leilani glanced at the clock on the wall again. Five after eight. Man, it was going to be a long day at this rate.

Okay. At least she had a full itinerary to keep them busy. First though, a few questions. She glanced at his cane, then back to his eyes. "How are you with walking?"

"Fine, I think," he said, adjusting his weight. "Like I said, I took my pain meds this morning and have another dose in my pocket in case I need it later. Actually, I think the exercise might do me good. My physical therapist back in Chicago is always on me to move more. Says it's the only way I'm going to get full function back and lose this someday." He waggled his cane in front of him.

"I may need to take breaks every so often, but I'm looking forward to a day in the fresh air."

"Okay then. Great." She started toward the front entrance, slowing her usual brisk pace to make it easier on Holden. "I thought we could start at North Shore, since the beach there is a bit less crowded than Waikiki and you can get to Diamond Head easy enough on your own with it being so close to the hotel.

"We can maybe grab a quick breakfast at one of the stands at North Shore too, then go see Honolulu's Chinatown markets, stop by the Iolani Palace downtown and visit the USS *Arizona* memorial, then end the day by hiking to Manoa Falls. It's short and mostly shaded, so it shouldn't be too tough for you. That should get you plenty hungry for the luau tonight when we get back to the hotel."

"Sounds great. Let's roll," he said, climbing into the hotel shuttle Leilani had commandeered just for their use today, then holding his cane between his knees. He seemed more relaxed now than she'd ever seen him, and Leilani had to admit she found him more attractive by the minute. "I'm all yours."

At his words, that darned awareness simmering inside her flared bright as the sun again, and she said a silent prayer of thanks that she was sitting down, because she doubted her wobbly knees would've supported her. There was a part of her that wished more than anything that were true, that he was hers, and if that wasn't terrifying, she didn't know what was.

She turned out of the hotel parking lot and wound her way through town before merging onto the H1 highway heading north, allowing the warmth from the sunshine and fresh air breezing in through the open windows to ease some of her tension away. His comment had been innocent enough and the fact that she instantly took it as more spoke to her own loneliness and neglected libido than anything else. Traffic thinned as they left the city behind. For his part, Holden seemed content to just stare out the window at the passing scenery, dark sunglasses hiding his eyes from her view.

Good thing too, since they were passing right by the spot where the accident had happened years ago. Man, she hadn't even thought about that when she'd been planning the itinerary for today, which only went to show how torn and twisted she'd been about this whole excursion. Now though, as they neared the junction of H1 and H2 and she veered off toward the right and the H2 highway, Leilani spotted a sign for the outlet mall close by and gripped the steering wheel tighter. They'd been going there that day, shopping for back-to-school clothes for her and her brother, when the accident happened. Her mouth dried and her chest ached as she held her breath and sped past the spot where they'd skidded off the road after impact, their station wagon tumbling over and over down into the ravine until finally landing on its roof, the wheels still spinning and groaning, the smell of gasoline and hissing steam from the radiator as pungent now as they'd been that long-ago day when Leilani had been trapped in the back seat, upside down, gravely injured, screaming for help while her loved ones died around her…

"Uh, are we in a huge hurry?" Holden said from the passenger seat, drawing her back to the present. "Speedometer says we're pushing eighty."

Crap.

She forced herself to take a breath and eased her death

grip on the steering wheel. Throat parched, her words emerged as little more than a croak. "Sorry. Lead foot."

Holden watched her closely, his gaze hidden behind those dark glasses of his, but all the same, Leilani could feel his stare burning. Her cheek prickled from it and she focused on easing her foot off the accelerator to avoid the unsettling panic still thrumming through her bloodstream. It was fine. Things were all fine now. She was safe. They were safe.

"Everything okay?" Holden asked after a moment. "You look a little pale."

"No. It's fine." She took a few deep breaths as a couple of cars passed them. "Driving on the freeway bothers me, that's all."

His full lips turned down at the corners. "You should've said something earlier. If this is making you uncomfortable, we can go somewhere else. I can see the beach myself another time."

"No, it's fine." She kept her eyes straight ahead, afraid that if she looked at him, he'd see all the turmoil inside her. "Look. There's a sign for the Dole Plantation."

Holden looked toward his window then back to her. "Should we go there instead?"

"Nah." She shrugged, releasing some of the knots between her shoulder blades. "It's pretty and all, but not very exciting."

"Not very exciting isn't always a bad thing," he said, shifting to face front again.

The hint of sadness in his voice made her want to ask him more about his injuries, but after her flashbacks a minute ago, now didn't seem like the best time. Instead, she drove on toward the beach and, hopefully, something to keep them busy and away from dangerous topics. The rest of the forty-minute trip passed without incident, thankfully.

Sure enough, the beach was lovely. Fewer people and beautiful stretches of sand and surf for miles. They grabbed acai bowls in Haleiwa Town, then headed over to Ehukai Beach Park and the Banzai Pipeline to watch the surfers shred some waves.

They snagged some seats atop a wooden table in one of the picnic areas lining the sandy beach and had excellent views of the massive waves crashing toward the rocks just offshore.

"Man, that's impressive," Holden said around a bite of granola, coconut and tangy acai berries. "Look at that. How big do the waves get here?"

"Up to twenty-five feet during the winter. We're at the tail end now, with it being March, but they can still get pretty big." She chuckled at a small boy running out into the surf. "Check him out. Can't be more than five and already fearless."

"Wow." Holden stared wide-eyed as the child held his own on the big waves right next to the adults. "That's amazing."

"Yeah. I remember being his age and coming here with my dad. I learned to swim not far from here at the Point." Sadness pushed closer around her heart before she shoved it away. "Those were good days."

"Really?" He blinked at her now, suitably impressed. "So, you can hang ten with these guys then?"

She laughed around another bite of food. "Back in the day, sure. It's been years since I surfed though, so probably not now. Though they say it's like riding a bike. You never really forget."

"Hmm." He finished his food, then tossed his trash in

a nearby receptacle, scoring a perfect three-pointer. He swallowed some water from his bottle, the sleek muscles working in his throat entrancing her far more than they should. "Well, I certainly won't be doing much surfing these days with my leg."

He rubbed his right thigh again, tiny whitish scars bisecting his tanned skin. From a distance they weren't as visible, but this close she could see them all. The questions she'd been putting off rose once more, but before she could ask, he slid down off the table and toed off his walking shoes. "Think I'll take a gander down the beach, if you don't mind."

"No. Go for it." She watched him head off, then finished her breakfast before standing to throw her own trash away. It was a beautiful spring day, not too hot or too cold, the scent of salt and sand filling the air. Above her, seagulls cried and leaves of the nearby banyan trees rustled in the breeze. She'd used to love coming here as a kid, building sandcastles with her brother, or cuddling on her mom's lap beneath the blue sky. She wrapped her arms around herself and kicked off her sneakers, venturing down to the water's edge to dip her toes in the bracing Pacific waters.

Lost in thought, she didn't even hear Holden return until he was right next to her on the wet sand, his cane in one hand and his shoes dangling from the fingers of the other. His dark hair was tousled and the shadow of dark stubble on his chin made her want to run her tongue over it, then nuzzle her face into his neck. She swallowed hard and stared out at the horizon and the surfers balancing on the crests of the waves rolling in. "How was your walk?"

"Good. Needed to stretch my legs after the car ride." He took a deep breath in and glanced skyward. "Hard to imagine your dad out here though. Never thought of Joe Kim as a surfer."

"Oh, he's not," she said without thinking, then stopped herself. Too late.

Holden was looking at her again, reaching up to lower those sunglasses of his so his hazel eyes were visible over the tops of their rims. "I'm confused."

A few weeks ago, she would've walked away, shut down this conversation with him. But now, today, she felt tired. Tired of pushing him away, tired of keeping up her walls so high and strong, tired of running. Leilani sighed and shook her head. "The Kims aren't my real parents. They adopted me after my family was killed in a car accident twenty years ago."

"Oh," Holden said, his voice distant as he took that in. After a few moments, he seemed to collect himself and stepped closer to her to block the breeze. "I'm sorry. That must've been horrible."

"It's okay," she said out of habit. Years of distancing people took their toll. "I mean, it happened a long time ago, when I was fourteen. I've moved on." And she had, at least in most areas. Work. School. Anywhere that didn't require true intimacy. Speaking of intimacy, Holden's body heat penetrated the thin cotton of her pink tank top and made her crave all sorts of things that were best left alone. She moved away and headed back toward their car. "We should probably get going if we want to make our eleven-thirty ticket time at Pearl Harbor."

He lingered on the beach a moment before limping after her. "Right. Sure."

* * *

Three hours later, Holden sat on the hard bench seat in the Navy boat shuttle beside Leilani on their way to the USS *Arizona* Memorial, glad for a break to rest his sore leg. Not that he would've missed anything from their day. They'd already spent time at several of the other sites within the World War II Valor in the Pacific National Monument, including touring the USS *Bowfin* Submarine Park, the Pearl Harbor Aviation Museum, and the USS *Missouri* Battleship Memorial, as well as walking through the visitors center, the Road to War Museum, and the Aloha Court. Neither of them had said much since leaving the North Shore.

Holden had spent much of the time trying to wrap his head around what Leilani had shared with him. Being a teenager was hard enough without losing your entire family. He couldn't imagine what she must've gone through back then, the grief, the loss. That certainly explained the pain he saw flashing in her dark eyes sometimes though. Also explained why she'd known so much about that seat belt law in the ER that day.

He'd wanted to ask her more about what had happened, but then she'd not really seemed open to it on the ride to Pearl Harbor. Once they'd gotten inside the park there'd been films to watch and audio tours, and now Holden had no clue how to broach the subject with her again.

Of course, then there was the fact that coming here, to the site where so many had lost their lives in another act of violence brought all of his own pain rushing back to the forefront. December 7, 1941, was a long time ago, and he hadn't expected it to affect him as much as it did, but there'd already been several times when he'd nearly lost it.

The first time had occurred when they'd toured the Attack museum, which followed the events from Pearl Harbor through the end of World War II, and he'd seen the delicate origami crane by Sadako Sasaki, a young girl of only two when the bomb had been dropped on Hiroshima. Her goal had been to fold a thousand cranes during her time in the hospital for her injuries, which according to Japanese legend meant she'd then be granted a wish, but she'd only made it to six hundred and forty-four before her death at the age of twelve. Holden's chest still squeezed with sadness over her loss. Her family had donated the sculpture to the museum in the hopes of peace and reconciliation.

The second time had been during the film they'd watched before boarding the shuttle to tour the USS *Arizona* Memorial. Hearing the servicemen and women and the eyewitnesses to the event talk about their fallen comrades and the horrific things they'd seen that day had taken Holden right back to the shooting in Chicago—the eerie quiet in the ER after the gunman had opened fire broken only by the squeak of the attacker's shoes on the tile floor, the metallic smell of the weapons firing, David's last desperate gasps for air as he'd bled out on the floor beside Holden, and the helpless feeling of knowing there was nothing he could do to stop it.

He forced himself to take a deep breath and focused out the open window on the gentle waves lapping the sides of the shuttle. The scent of sea and the light jasmine shampoo from Leilani's hair helped calm his racing pulse. This wasn't Chicago. They were safe here.

They docked a few minutes later and got out to traverse the new ramps that had been installed the previous year for visitors to the monument. The other passengers were quiet too, almost reverent at they stood before the iconic white stone structure. According the audio narration both he and Leilani were listening to through their headphones, it was built directly over the site of the sinking of the battleship *Arizona* in 1941 and to match the ship's length, to commemorate the lives lost that day.

Ahead of them in line was a group of six older men, dressed in hats and sashes from World War II. Some were in wheelchairs or walked with canes, like Holden. All of them were visibly shaken the moment they entered the memorial. Holden himself had goose bumps on his arms at the thought of the brave soldiers who'd perished that day with no warning, no chance to escape. He felt their panic, knew their fear, understood their need to protect others even at the cost of their own lives.

Lost in his thoughts, he barely noticed when the narration ended and Leilani put her hand on his arm. He leaned heavily on his cane, swallowing hard against the lump in his throat, and finally met her gaze. Her expression was both expectant and worried and he realized she must've asked him something. He removed his headphones and swiped a hand over his face. "I'm sorry?"

"I asked if you were all right," she whispered. "You look like you're going to pass out."

"I'm fine," he said, though he wasn't. Thankfully, a cool breeze was blowing in through the openings in the sides and ceiling of the stone monument, cooling him down a bit. At her dubious look, he gave her a wan smile. "Really. But could we just stand here a minute?"

"Sure." She moved them out of line and over to the railing, where the breeze was stronger, and the shade helped too. As the other patrons in their tour group made their way up toward the front of the memorial, where the names of all the people lost that day were etched into the stone, Leilani leaned her arms on the railing beside him and gazed out over the water. "Every time I come here it hits me. How fragile and precious life is. How quickly it can be taken from you." She shook her head and looked at the horizon. "Not that I should need the reminder."

"True." He watched the group of veterans approach the wall of names, most of them openly crying now, and he blinked away the sting in his own eyes. He never talked about the shooting with people he didn't know. It was still too raw. But for some reason, Leilani didn't feel like a stranger anymore. In fact, today he felt closer to her than he had anyone in a long, long time. He rubbed the ache in his right thigh and exhaled slowly before saying, "I shouldn't need the reminder either. Not after what happened in Chicago."

She looked sideways at him then, her tone quiet. "Is that where you were injured?"

He nodded, absently fiddling with the head of his cane. "There was an attack in the ER where I worked."

Leilani frowned and shifted to face him, the warmth of her arm brushing his. "Someone attacked you?"

Holden took a deep breath then dived in, afraid that if he stopped he wouldn't get it all out, and right now it felt like if he didn't get it all out at once, he'd choke. "A shooting. Gunman looking for opioids. Guy needed his fix. Came in, got past the security guards and opened fire when we refused to give him anything."

"Oh God. Holden, I'm so so—" she started, but he held up a hand.

"I tried to stop the guy. Well, me and my best friend,

David. We tried to take him down before he could hurt anyone, but we failed. I failed." He swallowed hard and forced himself to continue. "Took a bullet to my right thigh. Shattered my femur but missed my femoral artery, luckily. David was applying a tourniquet to my leg to stop the bleeding when the gunman shot him point-blank in the back. He died instantly. The bullet that pierced his heart tore through my left shoulder as it exited his body. I lay there, bleeding beneath my best friend's body, until help arrived. Longest hour of my life. I thought I would die too. For a long time, I wished I had."

Silence fell between them for a long moment. Leilani reached over and took his hand, lacing her fingers through his before giving them a reassuring squeeze. "How long ago did it happen?"

"Almost a year." The group of veterans at the stone wall turned to make their way out of the memorial arm in arm, a brotherhood forged by grief and remembrance. Holden used his free hand to swipe at the dampness on his own cheeks, not caring now what people thought about him crying in public. Hell, almost every person in the place had tears in their eyes it was that moving.

He took another deep breath, then hazarded a glance over at Leilani. "I don't tell many people about that."

She nodded, staring at the lines of people going in and out. "I understand. I don't talk about the accident much either."

Her hand was still covering his, soft and strong and steady, just like the woman herself. He had the crazy urge to put his arm around her and pull her into his side, bury his nose in her sweet-smelling hair, hold her close and never let her go.

Whoops. No.

He wasn't staying here in Hawaii. He never stayed anywhere long these days. Leilani deserved a relationship that would last forever, not a fling with a broken man like him. She deserved better than he could give. So he kept to himself and pulled his hand away before he couldn't anymore. They still had the rest of the day to get through and the luau tonight. Best to keep things light and not mess it up by bringing his libido into the mix.

They got back in line and saw the carved names of the people who'd perished, then they rode back to the shore on the shuttle before exiting the park and making their way back to their vehicle. A strange sense of intimacy, a heightened connection, had formed between them after their mutual confessions about their past, but Holden refused to make it into anything more than it was. No matter that his heart yearned to explore the undeniable chemistry between them. Leilani was off-limits, same as before. They could be friends, good friends even, but not friends with benefits.

Nope.

Now, if he could just get his traitorous body on board with that plan, he'd be all set.

"So, where are we going next?" he asked, once they were back in the car. He swallowed another pain pill, gritting his teeth against the lingering bitterness on his tongue, then forced a smile. They couldn't have a future together, but that didn't mean he couldn't savor the rest of the day.

"Figured we'd hit Honolulu Chinatown next, get some lunch, then head to the Iolani Place before hiking to Manoa Falls to round out the day." She grinned over at him before starting the engine and pulling out of their parking spot. "Sound good?"

"Sounds great," he said, ignoring the way his stomach somersaulted with need now every time he looked at her. He'd enjoy their time together, remember today and move on when it was over. No heartache, no emotions, no vulnerability. Because that's what he wanted.

Isn't it?

Except as they merged back onto the H1 highway toward Honolulu once more, the warmth in Holden's chest told him that quite possibly he'd already gotten far more attached to his lovely Hawaiian colleague than he'd ever intended, and the realization both thrilled and terrified him.

CHAPTER SIX

AFTER WANDERING AROUND the markets and arts district of Chinatown and enjoying a yummy late lunch of dim sum and noodles at the Maunakea Marketplace, they'd hit the Iolani Palace in downtown Honolulu before heading to a residential street just past Waakaua Street. Leilani parked near the curb and got out. It had been a while since she'd spent a day just enjoying all that her hometown of Honolulu had to offer, and she had Holden to thank.

She should also thank him for opening up to her about the shooting and for not pressing her about the car accident that had killed her family. In fact, she wanted to thank him for a lot of things, not the least of which was for helping her to relax and just breathe again.

Honestly, Leilani couldn't remember the last time she'd had such a fun, relaxing day.

No. Not relaxing. That wasn't the right word, given that her adrenaline spiked every time Holden brushed against her or leaned closer. More like exhilarating. She'd had an exhilarating day with him. Good thing the short hike to the falls would help to burn off some of her excess energy. Otherwise she just might tackle him and kiss him silly, which was unacceptable.

Leilani waited on the curb while Holden got out of the passenger side of the car, then hit the button on her key fob to lock the doors before they slowly started down the sidewalk toward the trailhead. He limped along beside her, looking better than he had back at the *Arizona* Memorial. When she first turned and saw him looking gray and desolate as a stormy sky, her immediate thought had been he was seasick. But then she'd seen the pain and panic in his eyes and feared an anxiety attack was on the way.

So she'd steered him over to the side of the space and heard his harrowing tale. Funny, but she'd always felt a bit isolated after the accident, as if she'd been the only person to experience such a violent and immediate loss. But hearing Holden speak about the attack in his ER made her realize that she wasn't as alone as she'd thought. Of course, she'd had twenty years to adjust to the past. For Holden it was still fresh, not even a year had passed.

Knowing what he'd been through made her want to reach out and hold him close, keep him safe from harm and soothe his wounded soul. Except she wasn't sure she could stop herself there, instead falling deeper into like or lust or whatever is was that sizzled between them.

She wasn't ready to go there, not now. Not with him. *Am I?*

No. It would be beyond stupid to get involved with the guy. He was only there temporarily, and even if he wasn't, he was her biggest rival for the job of her dreams—which she needed to remember to ask him about too. Amidst all the fun they'd had, she'd forgotten earlier, but now she needed to remember her true purpose for today. Find out more about him and why he was here, so she'd know better how to handle the promotion competition at work.

The fact that he looked adorable and smelled like sunshine was beside the point.

"It's only about a half mile ahead to the start of the trail. Will you be okay?" she asked, giving him some side eye as they continued up the sidewalk.

"I'm good," he said, flashing her a quick crooked grin that did all sorts of naughty things inside her. "I took my other pain pill while we were in Chinatown, so I should be set for the next six hours at least."

"Great."

"Yeah."

They continued a while longer in companionable silence, dappled light through the palm fronds above creating patterns on the ground beneath their feet. The neighborhood was quiet and peaceful, just the occasional yap of a dog or the far-off rush of the ocean filling the air around them. The tang of freshly mowed grass tickled her nose and a pair of zebra doves waddled across the paths not far ahead of them.

"Did I ask you about Tommy Schrader?" Holden asked at last.

"Yeah, you did," she said, chuckling. "This morning back at the hotel."

"Right. Sorry." He looked away. "Thanks for today, by the way. All the places you've taken me to have been great."

"You're welcome." She pointed to the right and a sign for the trailhead. "There's so much more to see too. Besides Diamond Head, if you get the chance you should check out the snorkeling at Hanauma Bay. The zoo and aquarium in Waikiki are nice too. Oh, and Kualoa Ranch on the windward coast. It's beautiful, with a private nature reserve, working cattle ranch, as well as the most amazing zip line ever."

"Cool. I'd love to see it sometime." He closed his eyes and inhaled deep. "Maybe we can take another day trip together."

Her chest squeezed and she gulped. She'd like nothing better, so the answer was no.

When she didn't respond right away, he hurriedly said, "Or not. I'm sure I can find my way on my own. I didn't mean to—"

"No, no. It's fine." Liar. Leilani felt lots of things at the moment—excited, scared, nervous, aroused—but *fine* definitely wasn't one of them. Still, she'd gotten so used to blowing off people's concern over the years it was hard to shift gears now. "I mean, I appreciate the offer, but I'd have to check my schedule and things are a bit crazy right now at the hotel too, so my parents need my help sometimes in my off hours and…"

He gave her a curious look. "The Kims seem like good people. You were lucky to have them adopt you."

Glad for the change of subject, Leilani took the bait. "Yeah, they're awesome. They were friends of my parents, actually. It was easier for me to adjust to living with them than it might've been if they were strangers."

He nodded and continued beside her onto the wide, black, gravel-covered trail into the rain forest surrounding the waterfall. "Like I said before, I can't imagine how hard that must've been for you, losing your family. And at that age too. Being a teenager is hard enough as it is."

"True." The light was dimmer in here with the thick foliage and the temperature had dropped. Leilani shivered slightly and was surprised when Holden moved closer to share body heat. The scent of dirt and fresh growing things surrounded them, and the low hum of the waterfall ahead created a sense of privacy. She'd not gone into detail about the accident with Holden earlier at the beach, but with everything he'd shared with her about the shooting, she felt like, for the first time in a long time, she could open up with him too.

They crested a short hill and reached the falls. One hundred and fifty feet tall, the water cascaded down the granite walls behind it, shimmering with rainbows in the sun. She looked over at him, her pulse tripping a bit at his strong profile, his firm lips, so handsome, so kissable. He was almost as dazzling as the falls themselves. To distract herself she asked the most mundane thing she could think of. "Why'd you go into emergency medicine?"

Holden shrugged. "I always loved science as a kid and wanted to know how things worked, especially things inside the body. I'm a natural problem solver and detail oriented. But I'm also restless and a bit hyperactive, so I needed to choose a specialty that took that into consideration. Trauma surgery ticked all the boxes for me." He smiled, his teeth white and even in the slight shadows from the trees around them, and the barriers around her heart crumbled a bit more. "What about you?"

"Well," she said, moving her ponytail aside to reveal the scar on her neck. "See this?"

He leaned in closer, his warm breath tickling her skin. She suppressed another shiver, this one having nothing to do with the temperature and everything to do with the man beside her. "Wow. Is that from the accident?"

"It is." Leilani took a deep breath, then exhaled slowly before diving in. "We were on our way to the outlet mall, of all places. It was a sunny day and hot. The sky was blue and cloudless. Weird how I remember that, right?"

"Nah." Holden took her arm to pull her aside to let another couple pass them on the trail. "I remember all the details about the shooting. What people wore, what the room smelled like, how the floor felt sticky under my cheek. It's what trauma does to people's memories."

She nodded, then continued down the trail once the other people had passed. "Anyway, our car was an older model. When the other driver T-boned us, it sent us through the guardrail and down into a ravine. Car flipped over three times before landing on the roof, from what the police report says." She blinked hard against the tears that threatened to fall. "My brother and parents died instantly." They stopped under a natural canopy of tree trunks entwined over the trail, and Leilani rested back against their solid weight for support. "I was the only one left alive."

"Oh God." Holden stepped closer and took her hand this time, holding it close to his chest. The steady *thump-thump* of his heart beneath her palm helped ground her and kept her from getting lost in the past again. "I'm so sorry, Leilani. How in the world did you survive?"

"Sheer luck, I'm pretty sure." She gave a sad little laugh. "Both my legs were broken, but I was awake the whole time. I still have nightmares about it sometimes."

"I bet."

After another deep breath, she continued. "The scar on my neck is from a chunk of glass that lodged there. It nicked the artery but kept enough pressure until help arrived. Otherwise I would've died like the rest of my family. The only reason I'm here now is the paramedics and the ER staff who helped me that day. So that's why I went into emergency medicine. Because of their compassion and to pay my debt to them."

"Wow." He slowly slid his arm around her and pulled her into a hug. She didn't resist, too drained from telling her story and, well, it just felt too darned good being this close to him at last. He rested his chin on the top of her head and said again, "Wow."

The stroke of his fingers against her scalp felt so good it nearly hypnotized her.

"That's why you knew about the seat belt laws, isn't it?" he asked after a moment, his voice ruffling the hair at her temple.

"Yeah," she said, pressing her cheek more firmly against his chest. "Seat belts and air bags would've made all the difference."

They stood there, wrapped in each other's arms and their own little world, until more people came down the trail and they had to step aside to allow them through. Once separated, neither seemed to know where to look or what to do with their hands.

For her part, it took all Leilani's willpower not to throw herself back into Holden's arms. But then, thankfully, her good old common sense kicked in, along with the warning bells in her head, telling her that no matter how tempting it might be to throw caution to the wind, she couldn't do that. Couldn't let him in because he'd either be leaving soon or possibly taking the job she wanted if he stayed. Both of which would only break her heart. And she'd had more than enough heartache for one lifetime.

Hoping for some time and space to get her head clear again, she started back down the trail toward the car, then waited for him to follow. "We should get back to the hotel so we can shower and change before tonight."

Holden stared at his reflection in the full-length mirror in his room early that evening and hoped he was dressed appropriately for a luau. Honestly, he had no idea what you wore to a party on the beach. Swim trunks, maybe, but that seemed a bit too relaxed.

He'd opted instead for a fresh Hawaiian shirt, this one in a pale turquoise color with small palm trees and desert islands on it and a clean pair of jeans. Flip-flops on his feet, per Leilani's advice, since it was the beach after all, and sand was everywhere.

His mind still churned through everything that had happened that day, all he'd seen, and the things he and Leilani had told each other. He still couldn't quite believe he'd confided in her about the shooting. He never really talked about it with anyone, outside of his therapist back in Chicago and occasionally with Helen. But telling Leilani about what had happened had felt different today. Scary, yes, but also strangely cathartic and right.

Maybe it was because of what she'd gone through with that awful car accident, but she'd never once made him feel judged or forced him to go further with his story than he was willing. The fact that she'd also confided in him had made the exchange even more special. From working with her the past month, he knew she was almost as guarded as he was when it came to letting other people close, so for her to open up with him like that meant something.

Then, of course, there was that hug at the waterfall.

Couldn't deny that had been nice. Amazing, actually. And sure, it was ill-advised, given he had no business starting anything with Leilani. Holden never knew where he'd be from month to month, let alone year to year. Beginning a relationship only to move thousands of miles away wasn't fair to anyone.

Trouble was though, his heart seemed to have other yearnings where Leilani was concerned.

She was smart, sweet and made every nerve ending in his body stand at attention. But there was also a wealth of vulnerability lurking beneath her sleek, shiny exterior. Sort of like him. She'd been through things, dealt with pain most people never experienced, and yet she was still standing. That took guts. It also took a lot out of a person. Made them more resilient, yes, but at a cost. He absently rubbed the ache in his chest, then grabbed his cane.

Enough stewing over things that would never happen anyway.

He left his room and headed down to the lobby, where he was supposed to meet Leilani. Dinner was served at sunset, she'd said, but there were plenty of other things to see before then. It was going on seven now and the sun was just nearing the horizon. People milled about the lobby, most heading out toward the beach behind the hotel where the luau would take place. He'd chosen his outfit well, considering lots of other guys were wearing similar things. The ladies mainly had on casual dresses or skirts and a few had tropical flowers pinned in their hair. From somewhere outside the strains of ukulele music drifted through the air, and the general mood of the place was festive and fun.

Being taller than most people at six foot four did have its advantages, and over the tops of the people's heads, he spotted Leilani waiting for him against the wall near the exit to the beach. He started that way, only to find his path blocked by one of the hotel staff, a pretty Polynesian girl dressed in a traditional hula outfit.

"Aloha," she said, giving him a friendly, dimpled smile. She reached up and hung a lei made of black shiny shells around his neck, then kissed his cheek. *"Pōmakia'i."*

Blessings. He'd managed to pick up a few native words during his stay in Honolulu and he smiled down at the woman. Lord knew Holden and Leilani could use all the good fortune they could get.

"Pōmakia'I," he said in return.

He stepped around the woman and continued on toward the far wall, stopping short as he got his first full look at Leilani tonight.

Seeing her earlier today in shorts and a tank top or as she was usually dressed at work in scrubs was one thing. Seeing her tonight in a short, colorful sarong-style dress made of native tropical print purple and white fabric was, well… *Stunning.* Her sleek black hair was loose, streaming down her back like shimmering ink, and that strapless dress hugged her curves in all the right places, ending above her knee and revealing just enough of her tanned legs to give a guy all kinds of wicked fantasies.

She looked over and spotted him, then smiled, waving him over. He blinked hard, trying to clear his head of images of them hugging near the waterfall, of him pulling her closer, kissing her, holding her, unwinding that dress of hers and covering her naked body with his and driving her wild with passion until she was begging him for more…

Whoa, Nelly.

He ran a finger under his collar, wondering when the

temperatures had gotten so warm. His pulse pounded and his blood thrummed with need, and man, oh, man— he was in serious trouble here.

"Holden," she called, "over here." The slight impatience edging her tone cut through his haze of lust, spurring him into action at last. He slowly limped through the people to where she stood near the open doorway. At least the spark of appreciation in her eyes as she took in his appearance made him feel a bit less awkward. She liked him too. That much was obvious. Too bad they couldn't explore it. If he'd had more time here, then maybe, just this once…

Helen's offer of the directorship position flashed back in his mind.

No. He couldn't take that job. Leilani wanted it. She'd be damned good at it too. Better than him, probably.

But if it gave me more time here in paradise…

"You look great," she said, her words a tad huskier than they'd been before. Or maybe that was just his imagination. Either way, the compliment headed straight southward through his body. "Like you belong here."

"Thanks," he managed, doing his best not to get lost in her eyes. "You look beautiful."

Pretty pink color suffused her cheeks before she looked away and gestured toward the outside. "Thanks. Shall we?"

He followed her out onto the cement patio, then down the stairs to the large grassy gardens spanning the distance between the hotel and the beach beyond. A line of palm trees designated the border between the two. Rows and rows of long tables and chairs had been set up for people to sit and eat, and along each side were buffet tables piled high with all sorts of food. Beyond those were other activities, like spear throwing and craft making. She led him through it all—the men weaving head wreaths out of coconut leaves, the women making leis, the young guys offering to paint temporary tattoos on the cute girls. All the hotel staff seemed to be participating, all dressed in native Hawaiian outfits—grass skirts for all with the women's being longer than the men's, elaborate neck pieces and headdresses, leis everywhere. It was walking into another world and Holden found himself completely enchanted.

"This is awesome," he said, accepting a leaf crown from one of the men weaving them. "I had no idea it would be so elaborate."

Leilani showed him a huge fire pit, where a whole pig was roasting beneath enormous banana leaves. The smell was so delicious, his stomach growled loudly. Lunch seemed way too far away at that point and he thought he could probably eat half that pig all by himself. "Don't worry," she said, as if reading his thoughts. "They've got more inside in the kitchen."

"Good, because I'm starving."

"Me too." She laughed, then took his arm, tugging him toward the front of the area, where a stage had been set up and currently a quartet of local musicians played a variety of Hawaiian music. That explained the ukuleles he'd heard earlier. Holden spotted Leilani's dad behind the stage and waved to him. Joe waved back. Leilani pulled Holden out of the way of a racing toddler, then kept her hand on his bare forearm, the heat of her searing his skin and bringing his earlier X-rated thoughts back to mind. They stopped near the best table in the bunch, front row, center stage. "This is where we're sitting for dinner and the show."

"Really?" He raised his brows. "Pays to know people in high places, huh?"

"It does." She winked, then pointed back to where the pig was roasting. Two burly staffers in native costumes had pulled away the banana leaves and were raising the whole roast pig up in the air with a loud grunt. The crowd applauded and Leilani leaned in close to whisper, "C'mon. Let's eat."

Didn't have to ask him twice. After loading up their plates with Kalua pig and barbecue chicken and *lomi* salmon and poi and fresh pineapple, they made their way back to the table just as Leilani's father took the stage as MC for the evening.

"Aloha! Welcome to the weekly luau at the Malu Huna Resort. Please help yourselves to the wonderful food and enjoy our entertainment this evening. Mahalo!"

The band started up again, joined by hula dancers, and Holden dug into his food with gusto. "This. Is. Amazing," he said around a bite of tangy, salty *lomi* salmon. The cold fish mixed with ripe tomatoes and onions was just the right foil for the sweeter pork and chicken. "Thanks for inviting me tonight. And thanks again for today."

"You're welcome." She smiled at him over the rim of her mai tai glass. "I love my hometown and am always glad to share it with others."

"It's great here. Seriously." He swallowed another bite of food, this time devouring a spoonful of poi. It was a bit like eating a mouthful of purple cream of wheat mixed with fruit. Not bad at all. Next he tried more pork and nearly fainted from the goodness. "Man, why does food never taste this amazing back on the mainland?"

Leilani snorted. "Probably because you didn't hike all over an island back in Chicago."

"True." He continued munching away as the band played on and more dancers joined them onstage. They were picking tourists from the crowd as well, but he kept his head down to avoid eye contact and not be chosen for humiliation. Finally, he'd had enough to eat and sat back, rubbing his full stomach and smiling lazily. "I don't think I've felt this full in forever."

"There's still haupia for dessert, don't forget." Leilani said, still eating. "Can't miss that."

"Nope." He sat back as a server cleared his empty dishes, then hobbled over to grab himself a plate of said haupia. It looked a bit like cheesecake without the crust, served on top of more banana leaves. He brought back two slices, one for himself and one for Leilani, then took a bite. It was good—creamy like cheesecake, but a burst from the coconut milk that was pure Hawaii. "Wow, this is really good too."

"Told you." Leilani finished her food at last, then pushed her plate aside and pulled her dessert over. "Speaking of Chicago, how exactly to you know Helen King?"

Holden almost choked on his bite of haupia but managed to swallow just in time. "She was a visiting surgeon at the hospital where I worked. We got to know each other there."

She saved my life.

He kept that last bit to himself, figuring he'd already told her more than enough about the shooting and there was no need to ruin the night by bringing it up again. "Why?"

"Just wondered." She shrugged, then watched the

dancers for a bit. "I'm interested in the directorship position, you know."

Ah. So that's where this was headed. He wanted to
tell her she had nothing to worry about, but then he
couldn't really. Could he? Even if he didn't take the offer
Helen had made him, there was the other issue of Helen
not feeling like she knew Leilani well enough to trust
her with that much authority yet. Maybe her temporary
stint as director would become a full-time gig, maybe
it wouldn't. Either way, Holden planned to be gone before then anyway. He tried to play it off with humor
instead. "I kind of figured, since you're doing the job
already and all."

"Has she offered you the job?" Leilani asked bluntly.
Yes.

"No," he lied. Helen had brought the subject up, but
he'd turned it down. No need to bring that up either,
right? Leilani watched him closely, her dark gaze seem-
ing to see through to his very soul and for a moment he
felt like a deer in headlights. Maybe he shouldn't have
lied. If he told her the truth now though, that might be
the end of all this, and he really didn't want it to be over.
Not yet. He looked away, toward the stage, without really seeing it. "Why do you ask?"

"No reason," she said, the weight of her gaze resting
on him a bit longer before moving away. "I just…" She
sighed, then faced the stage as well, her tone turning
resigned. "Listen, Holden. About what happened at the
waterfall earlier. I don't want you to get the wrong idea.
I like you. You're a good doctor, but I'm not looking for
anything more, okay? We can be friends, but that's it."
She took another bite of her haupia then pushed the rest

aside. "And as friends, I'd appreciate a heads-up if you decide to pursue the directorship, all right?"

"All right." He was still trying to wrap his head around the swift change of subjects and how she'd sneaked in the bit about the waterfall into the mix, like he wouldn't notice that way. Of course, his analytical mind took it one step further, making him doubt the connecting and chemistry he'd felt between them earlier. He shouldn't care and yet, he did. In fact, her words stung far more than he wanted. Which was silly because he didn't want that either.

No strings, no relationships. That was his deal.

Isn't it?

Holden hung his head, more confused now than ever. Maybe it was the fact she'd beat him to the punch that bothered him. Usually he was the one stressing that there'd be nothing long-term. Yep, that had to be it.

He shoved aside the lingering pang of want inside him and brushed his hands off on his jeans, doing his best to play it all off as no big deal—when inside it felt like a very big deal indeed. "If I decide to go after the directorship, I promise I'll let you know. And don't worry about earlier. Look, we shared some personal things, hugged. That was all," he said, trying to sound way more unaffected than he was. "No harm, no foul."

The band cleared the stage, replaced by a line of men with drums. Torches were lit around the area and the same big, burly guys who'd been weaving crowns and throwing spears earlier took the stage. A hush fell over the crowd as Leilani's father announced the fire dance. Much as Holden wanted to see it though, a strange restlessness had taken up inside him now and he needed to move, needed to get out of there and get some fresh air.

Get his mind straight before he did something crazy like pull Leilani into his arms and prove to her that he didn't care about the job, to show her that their hug earlier really had meant something, no matter how much she denied it. Talk about fire. There was one raging inside him now that refused to be extinguished no matter how hard he tried.

Onstage, the male dancers stomped and grunted and beat their chests in a show of strength and dominance over the flames surrounding them. Holden pushed to his feet and grabbed his cane, feeling like he too was burning up from the emotions he'd tried so long to suppress after the shooting, but that Leilani had conjured back to life all too easily.

"I need to walk," he said to her before sidling away through the tables toward the beach beyond, one hand holding his cane and the other clenched at his side in frustration. "Be back in a bit."

CHAPTER SEVEN

LEILANI SAT AT the table for a few minutes, brain buzzing about what to do. He'd not really answered her question about the job, but she'd told him point-blank where she stood with that, so yeah. She'd put her cards on the table, careerwise. The next move there was up to him.

Emotionally though, there were still a lot of things she hadn't told him.

Things like if he'd have kissed her at the waterfall, she'd have let him. Would have allowed him a lot more than kisses too, if she were honest. An old, familiar lump of fear clogged her throat before she swallowed hard against it. Much as it terrified her to admit, she wanted Holden, plain and simple. If she were honest, she'd wanted him for a while now. That certainly explained the awareness sparking between them whenever he was around. She sipped her mai tai and tried to focus on the dancers onstage, but it was no use. All she could seem to think about now was him. About how well they'd worked together on the surfboard kid's case. About how adorable he'd looked that morning, awkward but adorable. About all the things he'd shared with her that day and how he'd made her feel less alone. About how he'd kept up with her, even though it had been hard with his leg. About how he'd not given up or given in.

He was kind and smart and more than competent as a surgeon. And truthfully, she'd always been a sucker for men with brains and brawn. Not to mention his dreamy hazel bedroom eyes.

Gah!

A waitress came by and replenished Leilani's drink, but she barely noticed now. All she could think about was the hug they'd shared earlier at the waterfall. The feel of him in her arms, the heat of his body warming her, the thud of his heart beneath her ear, steady, strong, solid.

The long-standing walls around her heart tumbled down even further.

Holden had lived through horrific events, just like her. He understood her in a way no other man ever had. And he didn't treat her differently because of what she'd been through either, whereas all the past men she'd been with had acted like she was made out of fragile china or something once they knew about the accident. Leilani wasn't breakable, well, not to that extent anyway.

She resisted the urge to rub the uncomfortable ache in her chest—yearning mixed with apprehension.

The trouble was Holden made her vulnerable in a whole new way. Part of her wanted to put as much distance as possible between them, let him go his way and stick to her own solitary path. But the other part of her longed to go after him, to find him on the beach and tell him that she didn't want forever, but she'd sure as hell take right now.

He made her want to take risks again. And that was perhaps the scariest thing of all.

Also, the most exhilarating. She couldn't remember the last time she'd felt so alive.

As the fire dancers reached a fevered pitch onstage, a volcano of feelings inside Leilani finally erupted as well, making her feel reckless and wild. She wasn't ready for a relationship with Holden, that was true. Relationships meant ties and connections and all sorts of other terrifying things that could rip out a person's heart and shatter it into a million pieces.

But a fling...

Well, flings were another beast entirely. If he agreed, a fling meant they could have their cake and eat it too. Given that Holden would most likely be moving on to another locum tenens position and the fact he'd flat out told her he wasn't interested in a relationship either, meant he might be game for an affair. He hadn't ruled that out at all.

She downed the rest of her mai tai in one gulp then stood. Desire vibrated through her like a tuning fork and adrenaline fizzed through her bloodstream. As the fire dancers' performance ended to thunderous applause and her dad took the mic again to introduce the Don Ho impersonator, Leilani weaved her way through the tables and headed for the beach in search of Holden.

Once she was past the light of the torches at the edge of gardens, it took her eyes a minute to adjust in the twilight. At first she didn't see him, then she spotted Holden near the shore, silhouetted by the full moon's light, his cane in one hand, his flip-flops in the other.

Heart racing in time with her steps, Leilani kicked off her own shoes, then rushed down toward the water, toward Holden, her mind still racing with discordant thoughts.

He wants you. He doesn't want you. It's all in your head. It's all in your heart.

Whatever the outcome, she had to try. Felt like she'd die if she didn't.

Leilani stopped a few feet behind Holden, hesitating before saying, "I lied."

For a moment he didn't turn, just stood there, staring out over the Pacific as the stars twinkled above. She lived and died in those few seconds. Then he turned to face her, his gaze dark in the shadows surrounding them. "About what?"

Feeling both brave and terrified at the same time, she stepped closer and forced herself to continue. She didn't do this, didn't run after men, didn't pursue her feelings. But tonight, with Holden, she couldn't stop herself. She wanted him and she'd have him, if he wanted her too. "I lied, earlier." She fumbled for her words. "I mean not about long-term things. I don't do those either. Not after the accident. But I do want you. I mean I want to be with you."

Damn. This was harder than she'd imagined. She took a deep breath and forced the rest out before she couldn't say it at all, grateful the darkness hid her flaming cheeks. "Do you want to have an affair with me?"

Yikes. Way to be blunt, girl.

Holden blinked at her a minute, unmoving, looking a bit stunned. She couldn't really blame him. Her statement had been about as romantic as a foot fungus. But then he moved closer, tossing his shoes aside along with his cane, to cup her cheeks in his hands. His expression was unreadable in the shadows, but the catch in his breath made her own heart trip.

Then he bent and brushed his lips over hers, feather-

light, before capturing her mouth in a kiss that rocked
her to her very soul. Forget romantic. This was mind-
blowing, astounding, too much yet not enough. Would
never be enough.

Oh man, I'm in trouble here.

He broke the kiss first, the crash of the waves against
the shore mixing with their ragged breaths and the far-
off crooning of the Don Ho singer belting out *Tiny Bub-
bles.* For the first time in a long time, Leilani felt more
than just a sense of duty, more than pressure to succeed,
more than the low-grade sadness of loss and grief.

She felt needed and wanted, and it made her head
spin with joy.

Before she could think better of it, she slid her arms
around Holden's neck and pulled him in for a deeper
kiss.

Holden got lost in Leilani—her warmth, the taste of
sweet pineapple and sinful promise on her tongue, her
soft mewls of need as she pulled him closer, so close he
wasn't sure where she ended and he began. His lower
lip stung where the stitches pulled, but not enough to
make him stop kissing her. He pulled her closer still, if
that were possible.

Then the doubt demons in his brain crept forward
once more. He shouldn't be doing this, shouldn't be holding her like this. He was broken and battered, inside
and out, and didn't deserve a woman like her, a woman
who was as sunny and vibrant as the island around her.
A woman who'd overcome the darkness in her past to
forge a bright new future for herself.

A future he wouldn't be around to share.

He summoned the last remnants of his willpower

and pulled away—only a few inches, enough to rest his forehead against hers as they both fought to catch their breath. His hands were still cupping her cheeks, her silky hair tangled between his fingers, and her skin felt like hot velvet to his touch. But he had to let her go. It was the right thing to do.

He wasn't staying. He couldn't stay. He'd been running so long—running from risk, from commitment, from the past—he didn't know how to stop. Leilani deserved so much more than he could give, even temporarily.

"I—" he started, only to be silenced by her fingers on his lips.

"An affair. That's all," she said, her voice hushed as the waves crashed nearby. "No strings, no pressure. I want you, Holden. For however long you'll be here."

The words made his pulse triple, sending a cascade of conflicting emotions through him—astonishment, excitement, want, sadness. That last one especially threw him for a loop. She was offering him exactly what he'd said he wanted. No strings attached. Just sex, fun, a fling. But for reasons he didn't want to examine too closely, the thought of a casual romp with Leilani made his chest pinch with loneliness.

She pulled back slightly, far enough to look up into his eyes, her own dark gaze as mysterious at the ocean beyond. "I know it's crazy. I just…" She hesitated, shaking her head. "I like you, Holden. And this chemistry between us is amazing. Be a shame not to explore that, right? Especially if we both know the score."

Right, his libido screamed in response, but he needed time to sort all this through to make sure he made the best decision. Because the last thing he wanted to do was screw things up between them. They still had to work together during his time here. If things went south between the sheets, it could have direct impact on their professional relationship, if they weren't careful.

And Holden was nothing if not careful these days.

The reminder was like a bucket of cold water over his head. He took a deep breath and tried again to speak, "Listen, I—"

Her dad called out from the garden area in the distance. "Lani? If you're out there, Mom and I could use some help in the kitchen."

With a sigh, she stepped back, letting her hands slide from around his neck and down his chest before letting him go completely. His nerve endings sizzled in their wake and his fingertips itched to pull her close once more, but instead Holden forced himself to turn away and pick up his cane and shoes.

"Be right there," Leilani called back, staring at him in the pale moonlight. The question in her gaze prickled his skin. "Just think about it, okay? When's your next shift at the hospital?"

"Sunday," he said, shaking the sand from his flip-flops to avoid looking at her. Because if he looked at her now, there was every chance he'd throw caution to the wind entirely and carry her back to his room to make love right then and there.

"Good. That gives us a couple days to think this through. I'm working then too." After a curt nod, she started back toward the hotel. "We'll talk again then."

Holden stayed where he was, watching her walk away and wondering when in the hell he'd lost complete control of his senses because damn if he didn't want to say yes to an affair.

CHAPTER EIGHT

LEILANI SAT IN her tiny office at the hospital two days later, working her way through a backlog of paperwork that had stacked up over the last week or so while she'd been too busy in the ER. Today was slower, so she'd decided to tackle some of it while she could.

Well, that and she needed a distraction for the constant replays of her kiss with Holden on the beach and her brazen invitation for them to have an affair.

You shouldn't have done that, the commonsense portion of her brain warned.

The thing was though, Leilani had spent her whole life up to this point doing what she *should* do. For once, she was ready to go with what she *wanted* to do. And what she wanted was Holden Ross.

Even if the whole idea of opening up with him like that pushed every crazy button inside her.

A one-night stand was one thing but having to get up the next morning and see that person at work was entirely another. Of course, there wasn't any specific rule against dating coworker's in Ohana policies. She'd checked. But there was still the possibility that things could go wrong. And the last thing she wanted was to mess up her good reputation here by getting chewed up and spit out by the rumor mill. At least that's the excuse she was going with.

Truth was she was scared and looking for an opportunity to back out of the whole thing. Perhaps that explained why she'd been avoiding him since Friday night. Making heated suggestions in the moonlight was one thing. Looking that person in the eye again in broad daylight was quite another. So she'd kept her head down and her nose to the grindstone since their kiss. Because of that, she hadn't really seen Holden much at all since Friday night.

They'd passed each other in the lobby of the hotel twice, her on her way in, him on his way out. Between the crowds and her parents' watchful gazes behind the front desk, neither of them had said more than a basic greeting. And today, they'd both been so busy working and had barely had two seconds to say hello, let alone get into anything deeper.

So yeah. Pins and needles didn't begin to describe what she felt, trying to figure out what to do. Thus, she purposely put herself in paperwork hell to keep her mind off things best forgotten. She rubbed her temple and concentrated again on the requisition form nurse Pam had filled out for the monthly supply order in the ER.

She'd just ticked off the charge for two crates of gloves when a knock sounded on her door. Without looking up, she called, "Come in."

"Dr. Kim," Helen King said, "do you have a moment?"

Leilani's heart stumbled. She swiveled fast on her chair to face the hospital administrator, wincing inwardly at the mess her office was in at the moment. She stood and quickly cleared away a pile of folders and binders off the chair against the wall, then swallowed hard, forcing a polite smile. "Yes, of course. Please, have a seat."

"Thank you." The older woman, looking crisp and professional as always, shut the door behind her and sat on the chair Leilani had just cleared for her. Her short white hair practically glowed beneath the overhead florescent lights and her blue gaze was unreadable, which only made the knot of anxiety inside Leilani tighten further. Beneath her right arm was tucked a large black binder.

"I wanted to speak to you about a project that needs done here in the ER," Dr. King said. "I'd like you and Dr. Ross to work on it together."

Right.

Leilani nodded. She'd forgotten about Holden mentioning that with everything else going on. "Absolutely. Whatever you need, Dr. King."

"Good." The older woman sat forward and crossed her legs, placing the thick binder on her lap. "As you know, we're preparing for our JCAHO recertification next year and part of that is reviewing all the security protocols in the emergency medicine department. Since you've been with us for nearly a decade and are interested in moving into the directorship role for the department in the future, this would be a great opportunity to show me your leadership skills."

"Absolutely."

"Great. I'll send you more information on what needs be done and the deadlines. I've asked Dr. Ross to assist you because he handled a similar project at a different facility, and I believe he'll be able to provide good insight on the project. I've already spoken with him about it and he's on board with assisting you in any way he can. I'll need the project completed by the end of next month." She handed the heavy binder to Leilani, who needed both hands to support its weight. "The current protocols are in there."

"Okay. Wonderful." Leilani set the thing aside on her desk, then stood when the hospital administrator did. "Is that all?"

"Yes. That's all for now." Dr. King walked to the door and stepped out, then leaned her head back in. "And thank you, Dr. Kim. I look forward to your completed results. It will go a long way toward helping me decide the best candidate for the directorship position."

Leilani stood there a moment longer after Dr. King had left, wrapping her head around her new assignment. One month wasn't a long time for a project of that size, especially when both she and Holden had other job duties to attend to as well. But if it meant impressing Dr. King and potentially winning her the directorship, Leilani would get it done.

Of course, that meant another mark in the "Don't sleep with Holden column," since the last thing she wanted was for a potential drama between the sheets to jeopardize their new project together. And Holden and Dr. King were good friends too. Couldn't forget that. If things with their fling went south, then that could impact her chances at the new job as well.

Ugh. Things were getting way too complicated way too fast.

As she sank back into her chair, her chest squeezed with disappointment.

Her whole body still thrummed each time she pictured them together on the beach, the feel of his hard muscles pressing against her soft curves, the taste of salt and coconut in his kisses, the low growl of need he'd given when she'd clung to him tighter...

Sizzling connections like that didn't come along very often. Plus, she liked spending time with him, talking to him, just being around him. Their day sightseeing together had been one of the best she'd had in a long, long time. But was exploring that worth losing the future she'd planned for herself?

Feeling more on edge than ever, she pushed to her feet and headed for the door. She needed to move, to think, to organize the jumbled thoughts in her head before she and Holden spoke again.

But she barely made it through the door before she collided with six foot four inches of solid temptation, wearing soft green scrubs and a sexy smile on his handsome face.

"Hey," he said, his voice a tad hesitant. "I was just coming to talk to you. I'm on break."

Hands off, her brain whispered, even as her ovaries danced a happy jig.

"Good. Because I need to talk to you too. Dr. King came to see me about the project."

She gestured him into her office, then closed the door behind him. Perhaps discussing work would keep her errant brain on track. Except as he passed her, the smell of soap from his skin and his citrusy shampoo drifted around her and her chest squeezed with yearning before she tamped it down. He took a seat in the chair vacated by Dr. King, then set his cane aside.

"Well, on the bright side, the work should go faster with two of us working on it, at least," he said.

"True." She leaned her hips back against the edge

of her desk and crossed her arms over her lab coat and stethoscope. "I want to do a good job, since she said this will help her decide who gets the directorship position." Her gaze narrowed on him, trying to read past his usual stoic expression. "Are you sure you're not considering the job yourself? Tell me the truth, Holden."

A muscle ticked near his tense jaw and he frowned down at the floor. "I'm not planning on taking the job, no."

Good. One less thing to worry about.

Then he stood and stepped toward her and the desire she'd tried so hard to keep on low simmer since Friday rolled over into full boil again.

"Can we talk about something else now?" he asked, his rough, quiet tone sending molten warmth through her traitorous body. "Like Friday night."

Leilani squeezed her eyes shut and took a deep breath. "Yes."

When he didn't answer right away, she squinted one eye open to find him watching her with a narrowed gaze, his expression quizzical now, as if he was trying to figure her out. Finally, he took one more step closer and slid his arm around her waist, his hand resting on her lower back as she placed her palms on his chest. That same spark of attraction, of need, flared to life inside her, urging her to throw caution aside and live again, to take what she wanted from Holden and enjoy the moment because it would all be over too soon. She inhaled deep and hazarded a look up into his eyes, noting the same heat there, feeling the pound of his heart under her palms.

"If we're doing a project of this size, it would mean a lot of hours, a lot of time spent together," he said, his words barely more than a whisper. His hold on her tightened, causing her to bump into his chest. Her eyes fluttered shut as he bent and brushed his lips across hers before trailing his mouth down her cheek and jaw to nuzzle her neck and earlobe. "I haven't been able to think about anything but you since Friday."

She shivered with sensual delight, craving his touch more than her next breath, but that small part of her brain that was terrified of getting too close demanded she set boundaries up front. "Me neither," she panted. "But whatever happens, we can't let it interfere with work."

"Never," he vowed, his breath hot against her throat. "I promise you this thing between us will stay between the sheets. I won't let it get out of hand."

"I won't either," she said, not knowing or caring if it was true or not. All she wanted right now was his mouth back on hers. That's when she noticed his stitches were gone. "You got them out?"

"I did. Removed them myself earlier today." He chuckled. "Good as new thanks to you, Doc."

He kissed her again then, deep and full of passion. When he finally pulled away, she felt bewitched and bewildered and all kinds of bothered. Holden straightened his scrub shirt, then gave her a sexy smile before grabbing his cane. "What time does your shift end?"

"Four," she managed to say past the tightness in her throat. "You?"

"Six." He headed for the door, then turned back to her with a wink. "Come to my room for dinner. Number 1402. Eight o'clock. Don't be late."

Holden stood before the doors leading out to his room's balcony later that evening, wondering exactly what had possessed him to be so bold earlier in Leilani's office. Maybe it was the fact he hadn't been able to stop thinking about her since their kiss on the beach. Maybe it was the fact that after that day they'd spent together and sharing their most traumatic moments in life, he felt the bond between them even more strongly than before.

Whatever it was, he was now on a collision course of his own making.

He turned slightly to look back over his shoulder at the small table set for two in the corner of his junior suite, set up by room service and complete with a white linen tablecloth and a bottle of champagne chilling in the ice bucket. The lights were lowered and the single candle at the center of the table flickered in the slight breeze drifting through the open doors, casting a soft glow around the room. The scent of surf and sea surrounded him, as did the occasional notes of music floating in from a party somewhere on the shore. All of it should've soothed him.

But Leilani was due to arrive any minute and Holden felt ready to jump out of his skin from a mix of nerves and excitement. Now he'd made the decision to pursue an affair with her, he was second-guessing himself. Was this the right choice? Yes, he wanted her more than he'd wanted any woman in a long, long time, perhaps ever. And yes, she'd already made it clear that this was only a temporary thing, that she didn't do forever. Usually he was the one saying those words, and honestly, he wasn't sure how he felt about that. His analytical brain said he should be relieved. Leilani had taken the guesswork out of it all, taken the burden off him by offering a no-strings-attached affair.

Instead though, he felt torn.

Which was stupid, because a guy like him who was too scarred both inside and out to settle down for long had no business wanting more than a few nights in paradise. He should be happy with what he got because it could all disappear in the blink of an eye anyway.

Then there was the fact they'd now be working on that project for Helen together. And while he'd agreed days ago to do it, even before Leilani knew about it, now he was feeling a bit off-kilter about it. The fact he should've thought it through better in the first place bugged him. Going over security measures in the ER would be triggering for him, regardless of whether they addressed a mass shooting scenario. But really, how could they not, since that type of violence was on the rise nationwide. Not to address it would be wrong.

But at the time of the meeting with Helen, he'd been eager to please and wanted to help in any way he could to repay her for saving his life back in Chicago. The fact she'd tried to pressure him about the directorship position didn't help either. Now he had firm proof from Leilani that she wanted the job, and he wouldn't go near it, even if Helen wanted otherwise. Leilani deserved the position. He scrubbed a hand over his face, then fiddled with the hem of his black T-shirt. No sense getting worked up about it now. He had bigger things to deal with at present.

Get out and live a little. Trust me—you'll be glad you did...

Helen's words echoed through his head again and made him wonder if perhaps his old friend had assigned them both to this security project as a way of bringing him and Leilani together.

He snorted and shook his head. Nah. He was just

being paranoid now. Helen knew how squirrelly he was about commitment after the shooting, how he didn't want to stay in one place too long or form deep attachments. She wouldn't try to play matchmaker now to get him to stay in Hawaii.

Would she?

A knock sounded on his door while that thought was still stewing in his mind, making his heart nosedive to his knees. His pulse kicked into overdrive and his mouth dried from adrenaline, like he was some randy teen before the prom. No. Honestly, it didn't matter what Helen may or may not have intended. Both he and Leilani were consenting adults and they'd both made the choice to be here tonight. They were the engineers of their fates, at least in this room.

After a deep breath, he wiped his damp palms on the legs of his jeans, then limped barefoot over to the door to answer, his trusty cane by his side.

Leilani stood in the hall, shuffling her feet and fiddling with her hair, looking as wary and wired as he felt. She'd worn jeans too, soft faded ones that hugged her curves and made his fingertips itch to unzip them. Her emerald green top highlighted her dark hair and eyes to perfection and contrasted with the pink flushing her cheeks. The V-neck of her shirt also gave him a tantalizing glimpse of her cleavage beneath and suddenly it seemed far too warm for comfort.

Holden resisted the urge to run a finger beneath the crewneck of his T-shirt and instead stepped back to allow her inside. "Hey. Come on in."

"Thanks." She gave him a tentative smile as she brushed past him, the graze of her arm against his sending a shower of sparks through his already-overtaxed nervous system and notching the want inside him higher. Leilani stopped at the end of the short entry hall and stared at the table set up in the corner. "Are we eating here?"

"Yeah," he said, limping up to stand behind her, close enough to catch a hint of her sweet jasmine scent. Her heat and fragrance lit him up like neon inside, and his body tightened against his wishes. To distract himself, he concentrated on dinner. "Uh, I thought after a busy day, it might be nice to just chill and relax. Is that okay?"

She exhaled slowly, then turned to face him with a smile as dazzling as the stars filling the cloudless night above. "It's perfect, actually. Thank you for thinking of it."

"My pleasure." Holden grinned back, imagining all the ways he'd like to pleasure her, with his mouth and hands and body. He cleared his throat and gestured toward the love seat against one wall. "Make yourself comfortable. There's champagne I can open if you want some."

"What are we having for dinner?" She walked over to the table and lifted one of the silver domes covering their plates, then the other before turning back to him. "Salads?"

"I figured it would be healthy and—"

And would keep for a while in case we didn't eat right away and ended up in bed first.

He didn't say that last part out loud, but then, it turned out he didn't have to, because next thing he knew, Leilani had kicked off her sandals and was heading back toward him, the heat in her eyes heading straight to his groin.

"Good. Because there's something else I'm hungry for right now..." She reached out and traced a finger down his cheek, his neck, his chest, lower still. "And it isn't food or booze."

Before he could rethink his actions, he let his cane fall to the floor and pulled her into his arms, kissing her again like he'd been wanting to since their encounter in her office earlier, since the night at the beach, since eternity. It started out as a light meeting of their lips, but soon morphed into something deeper and more intense. Leilani sighed and ran her hands up his pecs to his shoulders, then threaded her fingers through his hair, making him shiver as she pulled his body flush to hers. "How's your lip?"

"Never better." He whispered the words against the side of her neck, licking that special spot where throat met earlobe—the one that made her sigh and mewl with need. Holding her felt like the most natural thing in the world. Even when she slipped her hands beneath his T-shirt and tugged it off over his head, exposing the scar on his left shoulder from the shooting. Usually, he kept it hidden, a dark reminder of a dark day, but now with Leilani, he wanted her to see it all, every part of him, the good, the bad, the damaged and the whole. In fact, the only thing he was thinking about now was getting Leilani naked too, and into his bed—over him, under him, any way he could have her.

She leaned back slightly to meet his gaze. "Sure you don't want to eat now?"

"Oh, I want to eat all right," he growled, grinding his hips against hers and allowing her to feel the full extent of his arousal. "I plan to lick and taste every inch of you, sweetheart."

She snorted, then wriggled out of his arms to take off her shirt and toss it aside, revealing a pretty pink lace

bra that served her breasts up to him like a sacred offering. He reached out a shaky hand to run the backs of
his fingers across the tops of their soft curves.

Then Leilani undid the clasp, letting the straps fall
down her arms before allowing the bra to fall to the
floor, where she kicked it away with her toe.

Oh man.

His mouth watered in anticipation. Man, he couldn't
wait to find out if she tasted as delectable as she looked,
all soft and pink, with darker taut nipples.

Unable to resist feeling her skin against his any longer, Holden slipped one arm around her waist, tugging
her close so her breasts grazed his bare chest.

Exquisite.

Then he went one step further, cupping one breast in
the palm of his hand, his thumb teasing her nipple as he
nuzzled the pulse point at the base of her neck, sliding
his tongue along her collarbone. Her moan and answering shudder was nearly his undoing. He smiled, savor-
ing the moment. "You like that?"

Her response emerged as more of a breathy sigh.
"Yes."

"Good." Holden dropped to his knees, ignoring the
protests from the muscles in his right thigh, and kissed
her belly button, her stomach, the valley between her
breasts, before taking one pretty pink nipple into his
mouth.

"Holden," Leilani groaned, her nails scraping his
scalp. "Please, don't stop."

"Never," he murmured, kissing his way over to her
other nipple to lavish it with the same attention, his fingers tweaking it as he licked and nipped and sucked until
she writhed against him, her head back and her expres-

sion pure bliss. Normally, he'd be unable to stay in such a position long, given his leg, but there was something about being with her that made his pain disappear.

The only thing that mattered now was this night, this moment, this woman.

Steering her by the hips, Holden managed to get them to the bed. His leg would protest the effort tomorrow, he was sure, but for now all he wanted was to get them both naked and to bury himself deep inside her. He'd stocked up on condoms in the nightstand, just in case.

Once Leilani's knees hit the edge of the mattress, she tipped back onto the bed, and he crawled atop the mattress over her. She ran her fingers up and down his spine, making him shudder again. It had been so long, too long, since anyone had touched him like this, since he'd allowed anyone close enough to try. And now that he had, he couldn't get enough.

Before he took his pleasure, however, he wanted to bring Leilani there first. Needed to see her come apart in his arms as he licked and kissed and suckled every square inch of her amazing body. To that end, he worked his way downward from her breasts, his fingers caressing her sides, her hips, before slipping between her parted thighs to cup the heat of her through her jeans.

"Holden," Leilani gasped, arching beneath him. "Please."

"Please what, sweetheart?" he whispered, nuzzling the sensitive skin above her waistband. "Tell me what you want."

"You. I want you," she panted, unzipping and pushing down her own jeans before kicking them off, leaving her in just panties. "Please. You're killing me."

He chuckled, ignoring the throb of his erection

pressed against the mattress. He was determined to make all this last as long as possible. He parted her thighs even more and positioned himself between them, then slowly lowered her panties, inch by torturous inch, until she was completely exposed to him. The scent of her arousal nearly sent him over the edge again, but Holden forced himself to go slow.

After kissing his way up her inner thighs, he leaned forward and traced his tongue over her slick folds. Leilani bucked beneath him and would've thrown him off the bed if he hadn't been holding on so tight. Tenderly, reverently, he nuzzled her flesh, using his lips and tongue and fingers to bring her to the heights of ecstasy over and over again. When he inserted first one, then two fingers inside her, preparing her for him, she called out his name and he didn't think he'd ever heard a sweeter sound in his life.

"Holden! Holden, I…" Her breath caught and her body tightened around his finger as she climaxed in his arms. This was what he'd been imagining for days, weeks. Hearing her call out for him and knowing that he was responsible for that dreamy look on her gorgeous face.

Once her pleasure subsided, he kissed his way up her body, stopping to pay homage to her breasts again before leaning above her and smiling at the sated expression on her face. She gave him a sleepy grin, then pulled him down for another deep kiss. Her hand slid down his chest to the waistband of his jeans, then beneath to take his hard length in hand.

He could have orgasmed just from her touch, but he wanted more. Tonight, he wanted to be inside her. Tonight, he wanted everything with Leilani.

Summoning his last shreds of willpower, he captured her wrist, pulling her hand away from him and kissing her palm before letting her go. "If you touch me now, sweetheart, it'll all be over and I want this to last as long as possible."

"Me too," she said, touching his lips. "Make love to me, Holden."

No need for her to ask twice. He grabbed a small foil packet out of the nightstand drawer while kissing her again, then climbed off the bed to remove his jeans and boxer briefs, putting the condom on before returning to her side. Supporting his weight on his forearms, he leaned above her once more, positioning himself at her wet entrance, then hesitating. "You're sure about this?"

"Absolutely," she said, pulling him down for an open-mouthed kiss.

Holden entered her in one long thrust, holding still then to allow her body to adjust to his size. Leilani began to move beneath him, her hips rocking up into his and he withdrew nearly to his tip before thrusting into her once more. She was so hot and tight and wet, everything he'd imagined and so much more.

Pain jolted from his leg all too soon however, and he couldn't hide his wince.

She must have seen it because, before he knew what was happening, she rolled them, putting him flat on his back with her over him. He'd thought having her beneath him was hot. Having her above him like that though, with the moonlight streaming over her beautiful face as she rode them both to ecstasy drove his desire beyond anything he'd ever imagined. Soon they developed a rhythm that had them both teetering on the brink of orgasm again far too soon.

"Oh," Leilani cried. Her slick walls tightened around him, her nails scratched his pecs and her heels dug into the side of his hips, holding him so close, like she'd never let him go.

Then she cried out his name once more, her body squeezing his, milking him toward a climax that left Holden stunned, breathless and boneless and completely drained in the best possible way.

He might've blacked out from the incandescent pleasure, because the next time he blinked open his eyes, it was to find Leilani laying atop his chest, drawing tiny circles with her fingers through the smattering of hair on his pecs. He stroked his fingers through her silky hair and for those brief seconds, all seemed right with the world. In fact, Holden never wanted to move again.

Finally though, Leilani raised her head slightly to meet his gaze, her chin resting over his heart as she flashed him a weary smile. "That was incredible."

"It really was," he said, the remnants of his earlier excitement dissolving into warm sweetness and affection. Then his stomach rumbled, reminding him of the dinner they'd neglected. She giggled and he raised a brow at her. "How about a picnic in bed?"

She rolled off him before he could stop her and rushed across the hotel room naked to grab one of the giant Caesar salads topped with crab and lobster before rushing back to bed. They got situated against the headboard, under the covers, then she handed him a fork and napkin before digging into their feast first. "My favorite kind of picnic."

CHAPTER NINE

THE NEXT MORNING Leilani blinked her eyes open and squinted at the sunshine streaming in through the open doors to the balcony. It took her a minute to realize that she wasn't in her own room. The warm weight around her waist tightened and a nose pressed into the nape of her neck, close to the scar there.

Holden.

She yawned, then snuggled deeper into his embrace, not wanting to get up just yet, even though she was scheduled for another shift later that day. Her body ached in all the right ways and sleepy memories of the night before drifted back. Honestly, after their first round of lovemaking, she'd expected to have been worn out. But man, there was something about Holden that kept her engine revved on high. The guy definitely knew what he was doing between the sheets.

Not to mention his stamina. They'd ended up having sex twice more. Once in the bed and again in the bathtub, just before dawn. Afterward, they'd finally fallen asleep together, wrapped in each other arms.

Being with him had been amazing. Awesome. Enlightening.

She'd expected his past and injuries to maybe cause

issues, but they'd found ways to make it work. In fact, some of the new positions they'd tried were better than she'd ever imagined. Plus, it was as if telling each other about their worst moments in life had opened them both up to just be present now and enjoy the moment. It was refreshing. It was energizing. It was addictive.

A girl could get used to that.

Except she really couldn't. Leilani sighed and slowly turned over to face a still-snoozing Holden. He would be gone soon, no matter how easy it might be to picture him now as a steady fixture in her life. Besides, she'd been the one to lay the ground rules between them at the start of all this. She couldn't be the one to change them now.

Could I?

She reached out and carefully ran her fingers along the strong line of his jaw, smiling at the feel of rough stubble against her skin. His long, dark lashes fanned over his high cheekbones and the usual tension around his full lips was gone. He looked so relaxed and peaceful in sleep she didn't want to wake him. Then she spotted the scar on his left shoulder and couldn't stop herself from touching that too. The thought that he might have died that day, been taken away before she'd ever had a chance to work with him, to know him, to…

Whoa, girl.

She stopped that last word before it fully formed, her chest constricting.

Nope. Not going there at all. No ties, no strings. That was their deal.

The happiness bubbling up inside her wasn't the *l* word. It was satisfaction.

Yeah. That was it. And sure, she liked Holden. Liked talking to him, liked working through cases with him.

Liked the way he looked, the way he smiled, the way he smelled and tasted and…

"Hey." His rough, groggy voice wrapped around her like velvet, nudging her out of her head and back to the present. "What time is it?"

"Early," she said. From the angle of the early-morning sun streaming in, it couldn't have been much past six, she'd guessed. "You've got time before your shift. We both do."

"Good." He stretched, giving her a glorious view of his toned, tanned chest before propping himself up on one elbow to smile over at her, all lithe sinew and sexy male confidence. "How do you feel this morning?"

"Fine." The understatement of the century. Heat prickled her cheeks despite her wishes. "And you?"

"Leg's a bit sore after the workout last night, but otherwise, I'm excellent." He pulled her closer and she snuggled into his arms, tucking her head under his chin.

"We should try and get some more sleep while we can," she said against the pulse point at the base of his neck.

"Hmm." He kissed the top of her head and her whole body tingled, remembering how he'd felt moving against her last night, moving within her. The feel of his lips on hers, the taste of him on her tongue. If he hadn't mentioned his leg hurting, she might've climbed atop him again for round four and give him something nice to dream about.

As it was, she lay there until his soft snores filled the air, letting her mind race through what was becoming more undeniable to her by the second. Somewhere between the hospital and their day touring the island and their post-luau beach kiss, she'd gone way past *like* with this guy. In truth, she'd fallen head over heels for Holden.

Her muscles tensed and she took a few deep breaths to force herself to relax.

Love was a four-letter word where Leilani was concerned. Yes, she loved her adopted parents and U'i. But what she felt for Holden was different—deeper, bigger, stronger. And so much scarier.

She didn't want to love him. He'd be gone soon, and she'd be left to pick up the pieces, the same as she had after her family had died.

Unfortunately, it seemed her heart hadn't gotten that memo though, dammit.

She fell into a restless sleep, dreaming she was back on the highway heading for North Shore, then down in a ditch with Holden trapped and with her having no way to help him. She'd woken with a start, thankful to find him still asleep.

Leilani eased out of bed to shower before heading back to her room to have breakfast alone and get ready for her day. She'd hoped time and space would help her forget about her foolish thoughts of things with Holden being about anything more than mutual lust, but that pesky *l* word continued to dog her later as she started her shift at the hospital as well.

At least the ER was busy, so there was that.

"I haven't gone for a week and a half," the middle-aged black woman said, perched on the end of the table in trauma room three. "Tried mineral oil, bran cereal, even suppositories my family doc recommended. Nothing."

Leilani scrolled through the woman's file, frowning. "Well, I see here you're on a couple of different pain medications. Constipation is a common side effect with those. Are you drinking lots of water?"

"I'm trying," the woman said. "But my stomach's cramping and it hurts."

"Yes, it can cause a lot of pain. We can do an enema here today and see if that helps." She made a few notes on her tablet, then walked over to a drawer and pulled out a gown to hand to the woman. "Put that on and I'll be back in shortly to do an abdominal exam, Mrs. Nettles."

Leilani stepped back out into the hall and closed the door before walking over to the nurses' station. Pam was there, typing something into the computer behind the desk. She glanced up at Leilani, her gaze far too perceptive.

"Hey, Doc." Pam smiled. "You look awfully refreshed for a Monday. What'd you do over the weekend? Have a hot date or something?"

"What? No." Leilani frowned down at her tablet screen. "I'm probably going to need an enema for the patient in Room Three."

Pam snorted. "Way to change the subject. Dr. Ross seemed to have a bounce in his step too when I saw him a few minutes ago."

Leilani prayed her cheeks didn't look as hot as they felt. "Well, good for him. That has nothing to do with me."

"Uh-huh." Pam sounded entirely unconvinced. "Well, I think two people as great as you guys deserve happiness where you can find it."

"Thanks so much," Leilani said, her tone snarky. "But can we focus on patients, please?"

"Sure thing, Doc." Pam finished on the computer then came around the counter. "Heard you and Dr. Ross are going over the security protocols. That's good, since your loudmouth MVA patient showed up here again last night. We've all been a bit on edge since."

Her gaze flew to Pam's. "Mr. Chambers came back?"

"Yep," Pam said, gathering supplies for the enema patient onto a tray. "Claimed he still had pain and wanted more drugs."

"Did you call the police?" Leilani asked, concerned.

"No. One of the guards got him out of here." Pam snorted and shook her head. "But the guy was shouting the whole time about how we hadn't heard the last of him."

Damn. That wasn't good news. She had a bad feeling about that guy.

"If he shows up again, please text me right away, okay?" Leilani said, heading back toward room three with Pam by her side. "Let's finish examining Mrs. Nettles."

Hours later, Holden sat in Leilani's office, going over the safety polices for the ER. So far it hadn't been triggering at all, he was happy to say. In fact, it had all been about as exciting as watching paint dry. If it hadn't been for her nearness and the enchanting way she blushed each time their gazes caught, he probably would've dozed off a while ago. As it was, he couldn't stop thinking about their night together. Or the fact she'd been gone when he'd woken up again.

Usually, he would've been fine with that. Save them both the morning-after awkwardness. But being with Leilani last night had felt different. Seemed the more time he had with Leilani, the more he wanted. Which was not good.

He'd agreed to her terms. A fling, nothing more. He wouldn't go back on that promise now.

She didn't do relationships and he was the last guy in the world anyone should get involved with. There were too many shadows still lurking from his past, too many demons he still had to conquer from the shooting before he'd be good company long-term for anyone. Some days he wondered if he'd ever be victorious over them and get back to the man he was before the shooting. Not physically—since his physical therapist assured him his mobility would only improve with enough time and hard work—but emotionally. When he was with Leilani though, she made him feel like he could heal the darkness inside him, could open his heart and love again. Truthfully, after being with her, getting to know her better, he felt pretty invincible all around. But that was just the endorphins talking. He knew better than anyone what a lie that false sense of security was, that false high of connection that made you believe in rainbows and miracles and love…

Whoa, Nelly.

This wasn't love. They'd had one night together. Things didn't happen that fast.

Do they?

"Okay," she said, glancing over at him. "We've knocked out most of the updates, and I put this one off until the end, but it's probably the most important. I understand if you'd like me to handle this one on my own."

"The active shooter protocol." He raked his hand through his hair and shook his head, hoping to expel the sudden jolt of anxiety bolting through him. He'd been expecting this, and still it took his breath away. He pushed to his feet to pace. He could do this. It was important. It could save lives. "No. I can handle it. What's the current protocol?"

"It's pretty basic," she said, her expression concerned as she looked away from him and back to the black binder in front of her. "The last time this was revised was three years ago and the problem has only gotten worse since then. This only lists sheltering in place and calling the police."

"Both of those are good, but it's not enough." Holden walked from one side of the ten-by-ten office to the other, then back again. His therapist back in Chicago had told him talking about what happened was good for him, better than keeping it all bottled up inside. Didn't mean it was easy though. Especially now, when he was still trying to process all his feelings from last night with Leilani. Still, this was a chance to create some good out of the tragedy he'd suffered. It's what David would've wanted. Perhaps he could find some closure too. Helen's suggestion that he help Leilani with the project made more sense taken in that light.

He took a deep breath, then began to talk his way through the problem while Leilani took notes. "We need to check out the Homeland Security website. They've got lots of good information and videos there to help us get the staff trained properly." He'd watched them all hundreds of times since the incident in Chicago, searching for reasons to explain why the shooting had happened and how to make sure it never happened again.

"Run, hide, fight are the three options basically. In the ER we've got both soft targets and crowded spaces to contend with." As he went over the whole "see something suspicious, say something" issue, Leilani gave him a worried look. He stopped his pacing and frowned. "What?"

"Nothing." She shook her head and scowled down at the paper again. "Pam mentioned that my patient from a few weeks ago, Greg Chambers, showed up here again last night asking for more pain meds."

"Did he make threats?" Holden asked, tension knotting between his shoulder blades.

"No." Leilani sighed. "Just lots of shouting and being generally disruptive. I told Pam to let me know immediately if he shows up again."

"Make sure to tell her to phone the cops too." He clenched his fist around the head of his cane. "The shooter in Chicago was after drugs. All the staff need to be trained on how to handle those situations, so they don't escalate into something much worse. If we'd had the proper training back in Chicago, then…" His pulse stumbled at that and he leaned his hand against the wall for support. Dammit. The last thing he needed was a panic attack. Not now.

"Okay," Leilani said, getting up and guiding him back into his seat. She stayed close, crouching beside him, stroking his hair and murmuring comforting words near his ear to keep the anxiety at bay. Slowly, his breathing returned to normal and his vision cleared. The ache in his chest warmed, transforming from fear to affection to something deeper still…

No. No, no, no.

He didn't love Leilani. They'd only known each other a few weeks, hadn't spent more than a few days together, had only had one incredible night. None of that equaled a lifelong partnership. It was just the stress of this moment, wasn't it?

Except...

Holden took another deep inhale to calm his raging pulse and caught the sweet jasmine scent of her shampoo. Damn if his heart didn't tug a little bit further toward wanting forever with her.

"Hey," Leilani said, standing at last and moving back to her seat. "I think I can find enough information on the internet to handle this section of the protocol from here. How about I put it together and then you can go over it all later to make sure I didn't miss anything?"

He appreciated her concern, but needed to keep going, if for no other reason than if he didn't, he'd have nothing else to think about other than the fact he'd gone and done the last thing in the world he ever wanted to do—fall in love with Leilani Kim. And if that wasn't a disaster waiting to happen, he didn't know what was. He swallowed hard, then shook his head. "No. Let's keep going."

"Are you sure?" She cocked her head to the side, her ponytail swinging behind her.

"I'm sure."

They spent the next few hours watching videos online and reading PDF manuals, coming up with training programs and protocols for the staff. It would take a while to implement everything, but at least they knew what needed to be done and that was half the battle.

The knots that had formed between Holden's shoulder blades eased slightly and he sat back as a knock sounded on the door to Leilani's office.

Pam stuck her head inside. "Sorry to interrupt, guys, but the EMTs called. They've got a new case coming in. Toddler caught in the midst of a gang incident."

"Be right there," Holden said. "What's the ETA?"

"Five minutes out," Pam said before closing the door once more.

"I'll help," Leilani said. "I could use a break from all this stuff too."

They moved out into the bustling ER again, and Holden tugged on a fresh gown over his scrubs and grabbed his stethoscope from behind the nurses' station while Leilani did the same. They met up again near the ambulance bay doors to wait.

The knots inside Holden returned, but in his gut this time. Hurt kids were always the worst. Plus, there was also the unresolved, underlying tension of the situation with Leilani. He cared for her, far more than he should. Love made you vulnerable, and that led to heartache and pain in his experience.

An ambulance screeched to a halt outside and the EMTs rushed in with the new patient.

"Two-year-old girl, bullet fragments in left lower leg from a drive-by shooting," the paramedics said as they raced down the hallway toward the open trauma bay at the end. The little girl was wailing and squirming on the gurney.

"Please, help my daughter," the mother cried, holding on to her daughter's hand. "I tried to take cover, but it all happened so quick."

"She's in good hands, ma'am. I promise," Leilani said, glancing from the woman to Holden then back again. "Can you tell me your daughter's name?"

"Mari," the mother said. "Mari Hale."

Holden helped the EMTs transfer the child to the bed in the room, then moved in to take her vitals. "Pulse 125. BP 102 over 58. Respirations clear and normal." The little girl gave an angry wail and reached for her mom, who was fretting nearby as the cops arrived to take her statement. Holden placed a hand gently in the center of the little girl's chest and smiled down at her. "It's okay, sweetie. I promise we're going to take care of you."

Leilani moved in beside him to examine the wound to the little girl's leg. "One four-centimeter laceration to the left inner calf. On exam, her reflexes are normal and there doesn't appear to be any nerve damage or broken bones."

"Okay." Holden stepped back and slung his stethoscope around his neck once more as the nurses moved in to get an IV started. "Let's get X-rays of that left leg to be sure there's no internal damage and to visualize the foreign material lodged in there." He called over to the mother, who was speaking to the cops near the entrance to the trauma bay. "Ma'am, does your daughter have any allergies or underlying conditions we need to know about?"

The mother shook her head. "Will she be okay?"

"We'll do everything we can to make sure she is." Holden typed orders into his tablet for fluids and pain medications for the child, then waited while the techs wheeled the table out of the room and down the hall to the X-ray room. The mother went along, taking her daughter's hand again and singing to her to keep her calm.

Depending on how deeply the bullet fragments were embedded in the child's leg and where, would determine whether he could do a simple removal here in the ER of if she'd need more extensive surgery upstairs in the OR.

"You okay?" Leilani asked, her voice low.

"Yes," he said. Shooting cases always brought up painful memories, but he was a professional. He pushed past that to do his job and save lives. The fact that Leilani thought maybe he wasn't all right chafed. He turned away to talk to the cops instead. "What happened?"

"According to the mother, it was two rival gangs settling a dispute," one officer said.

"Gangs?" Holden scrunched his nose. "They have those in Hawaii?"

"Yep," the second officer said. "Not as bad as they were back in the nineties, but a few are still here. The mom and kid live in Halawa. Lots of the gang activity centered there these days."

Holden glanced sideways at Leilani for confirmation.

"The tourism board likes to keep it under wraps as much as possible, but unfortunately, it's true," she said. "The housing projects in Halawa are filled with low-income families looking for a way out. Gangs exploit that and use it to their advantage. And every once in a while there are turf wars."

"And this poor kid got caught up in one," the first officer said.

"Is the mother involved with the gangs?" Holden asked.

"No," the second officer said. "Just in the wrong place at the wrong time."

Holden knew all about that. "Did you catch the people who did this?"

"Not yet," the second officer said. "Neighbors generally don't want to get involved for fear of retaliation. The mother gave us descriptions of the men who opened fire though, so at least we've got that to go on."

"What about her and her daughter then?" Leilani asked, frowning. "Will they be safe when they go home?"

"Hard to say," the first officer said. "We'll add extra patrols for the next week or so, but that's about all we can do, since we're understaffed as it is at the moment."

Deep in thought, Holden exhaled slowly to calm the adrenaline thundering through his blood. The last thing he wanted to do was patch the kid up only to send her and her mother right back into a war zone.

The radiology techs wheeled the little girl back in a few minutes later. Both she and her mother were a bit calmer now, which was good. Holden pulled the films up on his tablet and assessed the situation. None of the fragments were too deeply embedded. He could remove them in the ER and send them on their way. Good for the little girl, bad for their situation at home.

Leilani peeked around his arm to see the images. "Thank goodness the damage is only superficial."

"Yes," he said quietly. "But I hate to discharge them until the guys who did this are caught."

"Then don't." She shrugged. "Say we need to keep her overnight for observation. I can make arrangements upstairs for a room with a foldout bed so the mom can stay with her."

"Are you sure?" He gazed down into her warm brown eyes and his heart swelled with emotion. The fact that they were on the same wavelength with the kid's case only reinforced the connection he felt for her elsewhere too. Which filled him with both happiness and trepidation.

Leilani nodded, and Holden turned back to the patient and her mother. "Right. I'll need to perform a minor surgery here in the ER to remove the bullet fragments still lodged in your daughter's leg, then we'll want to keep her at least overnight to make sure she doesn't develop

any clots from the injury. Pam, can you get the procedure room set up for me?"

"Sure thing, Doc," Pam called, walking out into the
hall.

"And I'll walk you through all the forms to sign and
answer any questions you might have," Leilani said,
guiding the mother toward the door. She glanced back
once at Holden and gave him a small wink, then led the
woman from the room.

Holden smiled down at the little girl. He couldn't do
anything about the gangs out there, but he could keep
her safe in the hospital, at least for tonight. Plus, helping
his young patient and her mother gave him a break from
stewing over the mess in his personal life. He took the
little girl's hand and rested his arms on the bedside rail.
"Don't worry, sweetie. We're going to take good care of
you and your mom."

CHAPTER TEN

THE NEXT MORNING Holden was at the nurses' station, working through documentation on the charts from the patients he'd treated through the night. His mind wasn't fully on the task though, with part of it upstairs with little Mari Hale and her mother on the third floor. The two-year-old had come through the procedure to remove the bullet fragments from her leg nicely and there shouldn't be any lasting effects. He hoped that both the patient and her mother had gotten a good night's sleep in the peace and safety of the hospital.

Another part of his brain was still lingering on thoughts of Leilani. He'd missed sleeping with her last night, holding her close and kissing her awake so they could make love again. His body tightened at the memories of how amazing she'd felt in his arms, under him, around him, her soft cries filling his ears and the scent of her arousal driving his own passion to new heights.

But he shoved those thoughts aside. He was at work now. People needed him here. He needed to clear his head and get himself straightened out on this whole affair. No matter what his feelings were for Leilani, the thing between them was temporary because that's what she said she wanted. He refused to pressure her into any-thing she didn't want.

Period. Amen.

In fact, it was probably a good thing she'd been busy too since last night, dealing with her own cases and the security paperwork in her office, for them to have seen much of each other after dealing with the little girl. Im-ages of her from their day on the town popped into his head. She'd been so happy, so relaxed and in her ele-ment as she'd showed him around the island. He hon-estly couldn't remember when he'd had a better day, or better company. It was almost enough to make him want to stick around Hawaii for a while…

"Hey, Doc," Pam called to him from her desk nearby. "Dr. King wants to see you again."

With a sigh, he finished the chart he was working on, then shut down his tablet and stood. Helen probably wanted to check in on their progress on the project. "Be right back then."

"Happy Monday, Doc," Pam said, chuckling as he headed for the elevators.

The ride to the fifth floor was fast, and the recep-tionist waved him into Helen's office even faster. She looked perfectly polished, as usual, which only made Holden feel more unkempt. He patted his hair to make sure it wasn't sticking up where it shouldn't, then took a seat, setting his cane aside and folding his hands atop his well-worn scrubs. "Good morning."

"Morning," Helen said from behind her desk, watch-ing him over the rims of her reading glasses. She set aside the papers in her hands, then leaned forward, resting her weight on her forearms atop the desk. "So,

Holden. Have you given any more thought to staying here in Honolulu?"

He had, yeah. But not for the reason Helen hoped, so he fibbed a bit. "Not really. I've been busy."

"Hmm. Working with Dr. Kim, I suspect," she said. Well, it was due to Leilani, but not because of the project. "I've heard gossip that you two have been spending more time together."

He took a deep breath and stared at the beige carpet beneath his feet. Damn the rumor mill around this place. "I'm staying at the resort her parents own. We're bound to run into each other on occasion."

"Uh-huh." His old friend's tone suggested she didn't buy that for a minute. Helen sat back and crossed her arms, her gaze narrowing. "After everything you've been through, you deserve to be happy."

He hid his eye roll, barely. "Is this going to be some kind of pep talk? Because I really don't have time for it this morning. I need to get back to work."

"You know me better than that." Helen laughed. "I'm not a rainbows and sunshine kind of person."

Nah, she really wasn't. That's probably why they were such good friends. Helen told it like it was. A trait Holden appreciated even more after the shooting, when people treated him like he'd shatter at the slightest bump. Still, the last thing Holden wanted was relationship advice. "So, what is it you needed to see me about then?"

"I want you to think seriously about taking a permanent trauma surgeon position, Holden. That's what I want." When he didn't say anything, she continued. "Look, you turned down the directorship job, and I respect that. Having had a chance to go over Dr. Kim's credentials again, I think you're right. She is a better fit for the job. But that doesn't mean I can't use your skills elsewhere. You could stay in Honolulu, build a new life for yourself here. I can already see a change in you for the better since you arrived. You're more relaxed, less burdened by the past."

Holden took a deep breath and stared out the windows at the bright blue sky. Helen was right—he did feel better. Even his leg wasn't bothering him so much—well except for after his night with Leilani…

"Here," Helen said, handing him a job description. "At least look at what the job entails before you turn it down. I've added the salary I'm willing to pay in the corner there too, as an enticement."

Shaking off those forbidden thoughts, he focused on the paperwork. It was a good offer, with way more money than what he was making now, higher even than what he'd made back in Chicago. Plus, the benefits were great too. And it would allow him to put down roots again, if he wanted. Allow him to continue exploring this thing with Leilani too, if they both agreed.

But he wasn't quite ready to take the plunge yet. "Can I think about it for a few days?"

"Of course," Helen said, smiling. "Take as long as you need. I'm just glad you didn't flat out say no again. Now, get back to work. My next appointment should be here soon."

"Thanks." He hobbled to the door and opened it, stepping out into the hall before turning back. "I really do appreciate the offer and you're right. Staying in Honolulu would be nice."

He'd just closed the door and turned toward the elevators when he nearly collided with Leilani. He put his hand on her arm to steady her, then dropped it fast when he took in her stiff posture and remote expression. Not sure how to react, he fumbled his words. "Oh…uh…hi."

She blinked at him a moment before sidling around him, her tone quiet. "I have an appointment with Dr. King. Excuse me."

Leilani walked into Dr. King's office with her heart in her throat, Holden's words still ringing in her ears.

I really do appreciate the job offer and you're right. Staying in Honolulu would be nice…

Thoughts crashed through her brain at tsunami speed. When she'd first seen him in the hall, before he'd spotted her, she'd been happy, smiling, excited to be near him again. Then her brain processed his words to Dr. King. What job offer? The directorship? Did he want to stay in Honolulu? Did he want the same job she did? He'd said he didn't, but maybe he'd lied. Maybe he wanted to keep her off balance. Maybe he'd only slept with her as a distraction.

Wait. What?

No. Her heart didn't want to believe that, refused to believe that. But damn if those good old doubt demons from her past didn't resurface and refuse to be quiet. She ignored Holden's befuddled stare and fumbled her way past him and into Dr. King's office, closing the door behind her. She flexed her stiff fingers, more nervous now than her initial interview for the directorship position.

"Dr. Kim, please sit down." Dr. King gestured to a chair in front of her desk. "I wanted to ask you for an update on the security protocols for the ER."

Right. Okay. So, it wasn't about the job.

Why would it be, if she's already offered it to someone else? her mean mind supplied unhelpfully.

Leilani forced a smile she didn't feel and concentrated on explaining the pertinent details of the plans she and Holden had been working on downstairs earlier. "They're coming along well. We've worked through most of them already. The only one with substantial changes is the active shooter policy and I'm working on coming up with a substantial training protocol for the staff we can implement soon."

"Excellent," Dr. King said, fiddling with some paperwork on her desk, not looking at Leilani. "We'll need the details solidified by the end of the month to add to the rest of our recertification packet."

"I'll make sure it's completed." She swallowed hard, wondering if she should just come right out and ask about the directorship. Torn as she was about her feelings for Holden anyway, it would be better to know the truth up front so she could nurse her wounds in private. Her heart, her future, everything seemed to be on the line. If he'd lied, then she needed to know. Hurt stung her chest, but she shoved it aside. This was business. She had no right to be upset with Holden for taking the position out from under her. They were technically still rivals, after all. And the fact that she'd fallen for him anyway was entirely on her. Her heart pinched, but she pushed those feelings down deep. Personal feelings had no business in professional life. Honestly, if she'd been faced with the same choice, she would've made the same decision as Holden, wouldn't she?

Except no, she wouldn't have. Because she loved him, even though she shouldn't. It was so stupid. He'd never once said he wanted anything more than sex from her. She'd gone into their fling with her eyes wide-open and set the rules herself. No strings attached. The fact she wanted more now was her problem, not his.

Doing her best to stay pragmatic despite the monsoon of sadness inside her, Leilani cleared her throat and raised her chin. "Have you made a decision on the directorship position?"

"What?" Helen King looked up and seemed distracted. "Yes, I have, actually, Dr. Kim." Before she could say more, however, the phone on her desk jangled loudly, cutting her off. She held up a finger for Leilani to wait as she answered. "Yes, Dr. King speaking. What? Hang on." She covered the receiver and said to Leilani, "I'm sorry, I need to take this. Can we continue this later, Dr. Kim?" At Leilani's reluctant nod, Dr. King smiled. "Good. Have the receptionist pencil you in for another slot on your way out. Excuse me."

Right. Leilani left the office and headed back out to schedule her appointment then down to the ER, still stewing over things in her mind. She hadn't gotten the answers she needed from Dr. King, so it was time to be a big girl and confront Holden directly.

Determined, as soon as the doors opened and she stepped off into her department, Leilani made a beeline toward the nurses' station, her adrenaline pumping hotter with each step. "Where's Dr. Ross?"

Pam glanced up at her, her gaze a bit startled, and she took in Leilani's serious expression. "Exam room two. Stomach flu case. Everything okay, Doc?"

"Peachy," she said over her shoulder as she headed down the hall toward where Holden was working. She knocked on the door, then opened it to find him performing an abdominal exam on a middle-aged man. "Dr. Ross, can I speak with you a moment, please?"

"Uh, sure. Let me just finish with this patient first."

"I'll be waiting outside," she said, ignoring the curious look the nurse working with Holden gave her.

"It won't take long," he said.

Several minutes passed before he limped out of the room and followed Leilani down the hall to a quiet, deserted waiting area. "Is something wrong? Is it the little girl from last night?"

"No. The last time I checked in on her, Mari was fine." Leilani crossed her arms, her toe tapping on the linoleum floor to burn off some excess energy. "Want to tell me about your meeting with Dr. King?"

His stoic expression grew more remote, telling her everything she needed to know. "Uh, no, Not really. Why?"

"Because it would have been nice to have a heads-up that you were taking the directorship job I wanted." Her anger piqued at his audacity, standing there looking shocked and innocent when he'd gone behind her back to swipe the job out from under her. She should've known better than to trust him. Letting people into your heart only caused you pain in the end. And yet Holden Ross had gotten past all her barriers. Dammit. She wasn't sure who she was more furious with—him or herself. "That's the offer you were thanking her for, wasn't it?"

"No." The confusion in his eyes quickly morphed to understanding. "Leilani, that's not what happened."

"So, she didn't offer you the directorship?"

"No, she did, but I turned it down."

She couldn't stop her derisive snort. "You turned it down? I don't believe you."

A small muscle ticked near his tight jaw. "Well, it's the truth. She asked me weeks ago about it and I told her I didn't want it. Told her I thought you should have it. She agreed."

"Excuse me?" she said, battling to keep her voice down to avoid feeding the rumor mills any further. "Then what offer were you thanking her for upstairs? And why would she ask for your opinion anyway?" Then a new thought occurred, as bad as the previous ones. "Wait a minute. Have you been spying on me for her?"

The more she thought about it, the more it made sense. All that time they'd spent together, the day touring the island, the cases they'd worked together, their night in each other's arms. All of it was a lie.

He cursed under his breath, crimson dotting his high cheekbones now. "No." He raked his hand through his hair again, something he did when he was stressed, she'd noticed. Well, she'd be stressed too if she'd been caught in a lie. "I mean, originally Helen did ask me about you because she said she knew so little about you, but all I told her was that you were more qualified for the directorship than me."

"Damn straight I am," she said, on a roll now, hurt driving her onward, completely ignoring the fact he'd all but said Leilani was getting the job. This was about far more than work now, as evidenced by the crushing ache in her heart. She'd loved him, dammit. Opened up to him. Trusted him. And look what it got her, more pain and sorrow, just like she'd feared. "So, I'm just supposed to believe you now, that everything that happened between us wasn't just some ploy to keep tabs on me for your friend?"

"Is that what you think? The kind of guy you think I am?" That knocked him back a step and pain flashed in his hazel eyes before being masked behind a flare of indignation. He turned away, swore again, then shook his head, his expression a blend of resignation and regret. "Well, I guess that works out just fine then, doesn't it? I'm glad to know the truth because that makes my decision a hell of a lot easier." He wasn't trying to keep his voice down now, and the other staff started noticing them at the end of the hall.

"You want to know about my meeting with Helen King? Fine. For your information, Leilani, the job I was referring to upstairs wasn't the directorship. It was a permanent trauma surgeon position. Not that it's any of your business. And if you don't believe me then there's nothing else I can say. I thought what we shared together the past few weeks, the connection between us, spoke for itself, but I guess I was wrong. I was so stupid to think this would work, to think there might be something more between us than a fling. You said you don't do relationships? Well, neither do I. Especially with a woman who's so afraid to let anyone in that she pushes everyone away."

"Me?" She stepped closer to him, her broken heart raging inside her. "You're the one who's always running. Always hiding from your past. Don't talk to me about trust when you flat out lied to me."

"I have never lied to you, Leilani," he said, the words bitten out. "I—"

Whatever he'd been about to say was silenced by what sounded like a firecracker going off near the front entrance to the ER. The loud bang was followed in short order by screaming and people running everywhere.

Leilani started down the hall toward the nurses' station. "What's happening?"

Holden grabbed her arm and hauled her back. "I don't know, but I do recognize that sound. It's gunfire."

CHAPTER ELEVEN

TIME SEEMED TO slow and speed up at the same time as Holden's mind raced and his blood froze. Shooting. Screams. Sinister flashbacks nearly drove him to his knees. Another ER, another gunman. David, bleeding out on the tile floor as Holden lay beside him, too injured himself to help.

Oh God. Not again. Please not again.

"Holden!" Leilani shouted, struggling to break his hold on her arm. "Let me go! We've got to help those people!"

He wasn't expecting the punch of her elbow to his stomach and he doubled over, releasing her as he struggled to catch his breath.

"Wait!" he called as she ran off toward the front entrance, toward danger. "Leilani!"

"Use the emergency phone to call the police," she shouted to him before disappearing around the corner.

Damn.

Blood pounded loud in his ears, making it hard to hear as he dialed 911. After relaying the info to the dispatcher, he hung up, then swallowed hard and hobbled toward the corner, his breathing labored from the anxiety squeezing his chest. If anything happened to

Leilani, he'd never forgive himself. Regardless of what she thought of him now, he couldn't lose her, not like he'd lost David. He couldn't fail this time.

But what if you do...?

Teeth gritted, he pressed his back to the wall, the coolness shocking to his heated skin. He feared the shooter might be one of the gang members who'd shot the little girl upstairs, come to finish off the job. But as a male voice yelled, he realized it wasn't a gangbanger at all. He recognized that voice. Greg Chambers, the guy who'd punched him a few weeks back. The man Leilani had warned him about the day before in her office.

"Give me my opioids and no one gets hurt," the guy snarled. "Or don't and die."

Reality blurred again, between the ER in Chicago and now. The other shooter had wanted drugs too and he'd made the same threat. Made good on that threat too. Dammit. Holden cursed under his breath. The police were on their way, but what if they didn't make it in time? They hadn't been able to save David. No. It was up to him.

His analytical mind kicked in at last, slicing through the panic like a scalpel. Berating himself and "what if" thinking wouldn't help anyone now. Action. He needed to move, needed to find a way to take down Greg Chambers before he hurt anyone else.

Run. Hide. Fight.

Those were the words Homeland Security drilled into the heads of everyone who encountered an active shooter situation. Running was out, since the gunman was already here. Hiding would be good for those in the lobby, but not for Holden. He was the one person here who'd been through this before. He was outside the current hot zone and in the best position to surprise the attacker and possibly take him down and disarm him before the cops arrived.

More shots rang out, followed by screams and crying.

The unbearable tension inside Holden ratcheted higher as precious seconds ticked by.

Think, Holden. Think.

Eyes closed he rested his head back against the wall and thought through what he knew. Greg Chambers was an addict. He liked alcohol and drugs. Chances were good he'd be intoxicated now, since no sober person would attack an ER. If he was lucky, the guy's reflexes and reaction time would be affected by whatever substances were in his system. Holden could use that, if he could sneak up on the other man. He glanced down at his cane and winced. Hard to be stealthy with that thing. Which meant he needed to leave it behind.

Okay. Fine.

He set the cane aside, then took another deep breath, listening. Greg Chambers was still talking, but Holden was too far away to understand what he was saying. Then another voice, clear and bright, halted his heart midbeat. Leilani. As fast as his pulse stopped, it kicked back into overdrive again. If the bastard harmed one hair on her head…

Move. Now!

Holden hazarded a peek around the corner and spotted the shooter with his back toward the hallway. Saw Leilani near the nurses' station, hands up as she faced down the gunman while the people behind her cowered on the floor. She was so brave, so good, so beautiful and honest and true and he realized in that moment he'd do anything to keep her safe.

Even risk his own life.

After one more deep breath for courage, Holden inched his way toward the front entrance, doing his best to stay as silent as possible. His right leg protested with each step, but he pressed onward, knowing that if he didn't act now, it might be too late.

"Shut up, bitch!" Greg shouted, aiming his gun at Leilani again. "Sick of your talking. Give me my damned drugs before I blow your head off!"

"I can't do that, sir," she responded, her voice calm and level. Her dark gaze flicked over to Holden then back to the shooter, faster than a blink, but he felt that look like a lifeline. She'd seen him, knew he was coming to help. Leilani continued. "The police are on their way. Let these people go and put your gun down. You can't win here."

"Shut up!" Chambers yelled, his tone more frantic now as he looked around wildly. "I ain't going to jail again. I can't."

In the far distance, the wail of sirens cut through the eerie quiet in the ER. Holden spotted the two security guards near the automatic doors. One was down and bleeding. Holden couldn't see how badly. The other guard was kneeling beside him, trying to help his wounded comrade. Both guards' guns were at Chambers's feet, probably kicked there as the gunman had ordered.

"Give me the opioids and let me the hell out of here," Greg screamed again, waving his weapon around. "Do it, or I'll open fire. I swear I will. Ain't got nothing left to live for anyway."

He took aim at Leilani, at point-blank range.

"Bye, Lady Doc," Greg Chambers said. "You had your chance."

The snick of the trigger cocking echoed through Holden's head like a cannon blast. Adrenaline and desperation electrified his blood and he forgot about planning, forgot about strategy. Forgot about everything except saving the woman he loved.

Holden charged, wrapping his arm around Chambers's neck from behind and jerking him backward along with his weapon, sending the bullets skyward. He wasn't sure what was louder, the bullets firing from the semiautomatic or the screams from the people crouched in the lobby. Florescent bulbs shattered and chunks of ceiling tile rained down.

The muscles in his right thigh shrieked from the strain, but Holden held on, knocking the gun from Greg Chambers's hands, then flipping the smaller man over his shoulder and tossing him flat on his back on the floor. Tires screeched outside the front entrance and sirens screamed inside as the Honolulu PD SWAT team raced inside and took control of the gunman.

"Get off me!" the guy screamed, fighting and wrestling to get free as the cops handcuffed him and hauled him to his feet, reading him his Miranda rights as they walked him out the door. "I ain't going to jail!"

The adrenaline and shock wore off, and Holden slumped back onto his butt on the floor, breathing fast as he started to crawl toward the injured security guard near the door.

"Doc, we need help over here!" Pam called from behind him. "She's been hit."

His chest constricted and his heart dropped to his toes. Holden swiveled fast, his leg cramping with pain, to see Leilani slumped on the floor against the front of the reception desk, a blotch of crimson blooming on the left arm of her pristine white lab coat. She looked pale. Too pale.

No. Please God, no!

"Leilani," he said, reaching her. She frowned and mumbled something but didn't open her eyes. David had looked like that too, just before he'd lost consciousness. He'd never woken up again.

No. No, no, no. I won't fail this time. I can't fail this time. Please don't let me fail this time.

His hands shook as he carefully slipped her arm from the lab coat then pushed up the sleeve of her shirt. From the looks of it, the bullet had passed clean through. It had also passed perilously close to her brachial artery. Years of medical training drowned out his anxiety and emotional turmoil and spurred him into action once more. "Check her vitals. Order six units of blood on standby, in case she's hypotensive. We need an O2 Sat and X-rays to see the damage. Let's move, people."

While the residents dealt with the wounded guard and the other patients, Holden stuck by Leilani's side. He held her hand as they raced toward trauma bay one, refusing to let go, even as Helen King ran into the room and took over.

"Holden, tell me what we've got," she said as she did her own exam of Leilani's wounds. He recited back what he knew and what he'd ordered, all the while still clutching her too-cold fingers. When he was done, Helen came over and put her hands on his shoulders, shaking him slightly. "You're in shock, Dr. Ross. I've got her. Go and sit in the waiting room. You look like you're ready to pass out. You saved the lives of a lot of people today. You're a hero. Now go rest and talk to the cops."

Pam took Holden's arm and led him back toward the front entrance and helped him into a chair. He couldn't seem to stop shaking. "I can't lose her," he said to Pam. "I can't."

"She's in the best care possible, Doc. You know that." Pam shoved a cup of water into his hands before heading back toward the trauma bay. "I'll keep you posted on her condition."

A while later the cops took his statement, then left him alone with his thoughts. Holden tipped his head back to stare at the bullet holes in the ceiling and swallowed hard against the lump in his throat.

You saved the lives of a lot of people today. You're a hero.

Helen's words looped in his head but rang hollow in his aching heart.

He didn't want to be a hero. He just wanted Leilani alive and well again.

Leilani blinked her eyes open slowly, squinting into the too-bright sunshine streaming in through the windows of her room at the hotel. Except...

She frowned. The windows were on the wrong side of the room. And where were the curtains? And what was that smell? Sharp, antiseptic. Not floor cleaner or bleach, but familiar, like...

Oh God!

Head fuzzy from pain meds, memories slowly began to resurface.

Gunshots, Holden tackling the shooter, shouting, screams, a sharp burst of pain then darkness...

She moaned and tried to sit up only to be held down by the IV, tubes and wires connecting her to the monitors beside her bed. Her left arm ached like hell and her mouth felt dry as cotton.

"Welcome back, Dr. Kim," a woman's voice said from nearby. Leilani blinked hard and turned her head on the pillow to see Dr. King at the counter across the room. "How are you feeling?"

"Like crap," she mumbled, trying to scoot up farther in her hospital bed and failing. The whole scenario brought back too many memories from after the car accident for her comfort. "What's going on? Where's Holden?"

"He's fine. Should be returning to your bedside shortly," Dr. King said, moving to check the monitors attached to the blood pressure cuff and the pulse ox on Leilani's finger. "I made him go home to sleep and shower. Otherwise he hasn't left your side since the surgery."

"Surgery?" The beginnings of a headache throbbed behind Leilani's temples as she tried to recall more about what had occurred in the ER. "I had surgery?" She glanced down at the bandages wrapping her left bicep. "Who operated?"

"Yours truly." Dr. King smiled, then adjusted the IV drip settings on the machine. "Holden was a bit too close to the situation to handle it. And he was exhausted after taking down that gunman."

That much Leilani did remember. Considering what he'd been through, his actions had taken a tremendous amount of courage. He'd been a hero, saving her and countless other people. She ached to hold him and thank him for all he'd done, to beg him to forgive her for accusing him of stealing her job. He hadn't stolen anything. Except her heart.

"Anyway, I had to make sure you healed up nicely. Can't have my new Director of Emergency Medicine less than healthy." Dr. King stood near the end of the bed as Leilani took that in. "If you still want the position, that is."

"I…" She swallowed hard. "Yes, I want it. But what about Holden?"

"What about him?" Holden said from the doorway. Limping in, he set his cane aside, then took a seat in the chair at her bedside. "You look better now. Not so pale."

"Her vitals are good," Dr. King said. "And her wound is healing nicely. I'm just going to pop out for a minute. Dr. Kim, we can discuss your new position further once you're back to work."

An awkward silence descended once the door closed behind Dr. King, leaving Leilani and Holden alone in the room.

"So, I guess I should thank you," Leilani said at last.

"For what?" Holden frowned.

"For saving my life."

He gave a derisive snort. "I didn't save anything. In fact, I'm the reason you got shot in the first place. After all the research I did into active shooter situations, I should've known better than to tackle a man with a weapon."

"What?" Now it was her turn to scowl. "You're kidding, right? I don't remember everything that happened in the ER, but I do remember you taking that guy down. If anyone's at fault for me getting shot, it's Greg Chambers. You were a her—"

Holden help up a hand to stop her. "Please don't say hero. That's the last thing I am."

Leilani ignored the pain in her left arm this time and shoved higher in her bed to put them closer to eye level. "Well, whatever you want to call yourself, you saved a lot of lives down there and I'm grateful to you." She exhaled slowly and fiddled with the edge of the sheet with her right hand. "And I'm sorry."

"Sorry?" His expression turned confused. "What do you have to be sorry for?"

"For accusing you of stealing the directorship job. That was stupid of me. I should have believed you." She shook her head and gave a sad little chuckle. "I don't know why I didn't, except that I've been a mess emotionally since the luau and then that night we spent together and I took it out on you, and…" She shrugged, looking anywhere but at him. "I'm sorry."

"It's okay. I haven't exactly been thinking clearly myself since that night." He sighed and glanced toward the windows, giving her a view of his handsome profile. His hair was still damp from his shower and his navy blue polo shirt clung to his muscled torso like a second skin. Leilani bit her lip. He really was the most gorgeous man she'd ever seen, even with the dark circles under his eyes and the lines of tension around his mouth. She longed to trace her fingers down his cheek and kiss away his stress but didn't dare. Not until they hashed this out between them.

"Look, Leilani." His deep voice did way more than the meds to ease her aches and pains. "I know we agreed to just a fling, but the thing is, I don't think I can do that anymore."

"Oh." Her pulse stumbled and the monitor beeped

loud. Apparently, she'd misread the situation entirely. Just because she'd fallen head over heels for the guy didn't mean he felt the same for her. She should have kept her barriers up, should have known better. "Don't worry about it," she said, doing her best to act like it wasn't a big deal and failing miserably as tears stung the back of her eyes. Leilani blinked hard to keep them at bay, but her vision clouded despite her wishes. "We can go back to just being colleagues. Probably better that way since we'll be working together permanently."

"Yeah," he said absently. Then his attention snapped to her and his scowl deepened. "No. That's not what I meant."

"You mean you're not taking the trauma surgeon job?" she asked, confused.

"No. I am. I just… I don't want to be your friend, Leilani." Holden reached through the bedrail to take her hand, careful of her injuries. "What I mean to say is that I want to be way more than just your friend." He sighed and stared down at their entwined fingers. "I know I promised to just have a fling, no strings attached, but I can't do that anymore because I fell in love with you."

Stunned, she took a deep breath, her pulse accelerating once more. "Uh…"

"No. Let me finish, please." He exhaled slowly, his broad shoulders slumping. "You were right. I was running. I've been running since I left Chicago. Too afraid of getting hurt again to settle down anywhere. I never wanted to get that close to anyone again. Losing my best friend, David, nearly killed me, even more than the bullets did." He gave her fingers a gentle squeeze. "But then I met you. You were so full of life, so vibrant and smart and funny and kind. You were everything I didn't know

I needed. You healed me, from the inside out. Showed me I could laugh again, love again. So no, I can't go back to just having a fling with you, Leilani Kim. Because I want more. So much more. If you'll have me."

She sniffled, her tears flowing freely now. "You're the one who healed me, Holden. I thought I'd gotten over the accident that took my family all those years ago, but I'd just walled myself off, thinking that not caring too deeply would keep me safe. All that did though was make me lonely. You opened my heart again." She laughed, then winced when the movement hurt her arm. "I love you too, Holden Ross."

"You do?" His sweet, hesitant smile made her breath catch.

"I do."

He leaned closer to brush his lips across hers, and she let go of his hand to slip her fingers behind his neck to keep him close.

"I'm glad you're staying in Hawaii," she said at last, after he'd pulled back slightly.

"Me too." He nuzzled his nose against hers. "Does this mean we're officially dating?"

"I believe it does, Dr. Ross," Leilani said, winking. "The rumor mill will be all abuzz."

"Good, Dr. Kim." Holden kissed her again. "Give them something new to talk about."

CHAPTER TWELVE

One year later...

"WHAT DO WE have coming in?" Leilani asked, tugging on a fresh gown and heading toward the ambulance bay entrance.

Nurse Pam was waiting there for her, already geared up. "Per the EMTs, it was a rollover accident on the H1. Family of five. ETA two minutes."

Not exactly how she'd expected to spend the morning of her wedding day, but the ER had been short-staffed and as Director of Emergency Medicine, it was her duty to fill in when needed. Besides, it helped her stress levels to keep busy, since all the planning was done and all she had left to do was show up and marry the man of her dreams.

First though, it seemed like an ironic twist of fate that the last case she worked as a single woman was a rollover. Her biological family hadn't survived their similar accident, but today, she planned to do all she could to ensure history did not repeat itself.

Two ambulances screeched to a halt outside and soon the automatic doors whooshed open as five gurneys were wheeled in by three sets of paramedics. The

trauma surgeon on call—not Holden, thank goodness—
and a resident took the mother and son and the son's
girlfriend. Leilani and another resident took the father
and the daughter.

"You're in good hands, sir. Just lie still and let us do
all the work, okay?" she said to the father as they raced
for an open trauma bay. Then she focused on the EMT
racing along on the other side of the gurney. "Rundown,
please."

"Car rolled five times. Wife was driving," the EMT
said.

"I just remember coming around the bend and that
other car slammed into us. Then rolling and rolling."

"It was so scary," the daughter said as they transferred
her to a bed adjacent to the one her father was on, her
voice shaky with tears. "My first car accident. With the
four people I love most."

Leilani's heart squeezed with sympathy. Twenty-one
years ago, she'd experienced her first car accident too.
Worst day of her life. Funny how life worked, because
now—today—would be the best day ever. Once her shift
was over, of course. She rolled her left shoulder to ease
the ache in her bicep, then began taking the father's
vitals while the resident working alongside her in the
trauma bay did the same with the daughter.

"Do you remember what happened, sir?" Leilani
asked the father.

"I remember my life flashing before my eyes," he
said, his voice husky with emotion. "I remember glass
flying and people screaming, then everything stopped.
I'm just glad we're all still alive."

"Me too, sir," she said, swallowing against an unexpected lump of gratitude in her throat. "Me too."

"Patient is complaining of abdominal pain," the resident called over to Leilani. "I'd like to get an ultrasound to rule out internal injuries or bleeding."

"Do it," Leilani said before continuing her own exam on the father. "Where are you experiencing pain, sir?"

"My neck is killing me." He lifted his arm to point at his throat, then winced. "My chest hurts too. How are my wife and son? His girlfriend?"

"As far as I know, they're doing fine, but I'll be sure to check on that for you as soon as we get you set up here." She finished checking his vitals and rattled them off to Pam to enter into the computer, then carefully removed the plastic neck brace the EMTs had applied and examined the man's neck while a tech wheeled in an ultrasound machine for the daughter. "After you finish with that patient, I'll need a cardiac ultrasound over here too for the father, please. He's complaining of chest pain and has a history of high blood pressure and arteriosclerosis. Rule out any issues there, please. While we wait, let's see if CT can work him in for an emergency C-spine. I'm concerned about intracranial bleeding or neck fractures."

"Sure thing, Doc," Pam said, setting the tablet aside. "Keep an eye on your time too, Dr. Kim. Don't want to be late for your big day."

"I will. Thanks." She smiled at the nurse, then turned back to her patient. "Sir, we're going to get some tests done on you to make sure there are no underlying conditions going on I can't see on exam. Some films of your neck and head and also an ultrasound of your heart." She looked up as two techs came in to wheel her patient to radiology for his CT scan. "While you're doing that, I'll check in on the status of your family members, okay?"

"Okay." The father reached out and grasped Leilani's hand. "Thank you, Doctor."

"You're most welcome," she said, smiling.

The EMTs were still hanging out in the hall when she headed toward the other trauma bay to check on the mother and son and his girlfriend. One of the EMTs stopped her and showed her a picture he'd snapped at the accident scene of the mashed-up SUV lying on its side in a ditch. "The way that car looked, I'm surprised they all walked away. It's a miracle," the EMT said.

"It is." Leilani nodded, then headed for trauma bay two. "But miracles are what we specialize in around here."

She was living proof of that. She was also proof that you could not only survive the worst thing possible, you could thrive after it. Thanks to her wonderful adopted family, and Holden, who'd taught her how to love again. Her heart swelled with joy as she walked into the room where the son and his girlfriend were now sitting up and chatting while his mother gave her statement to a police officer. They appeared bruised and a bit rattled, but nothing too serious.

"I drive that route every day from our house," the mother said to the cop. "We were on our way home to watch a football game. That didn't work out so well." She sniffled. "When I saw that other car coming at us, I didn't know what to do. I didn't want him to hit us head-on, so I swerved to the left and my poor husband took the brunt." She looked up and spotted Leilani, her expression frantic. "Is he okay? Is my husband okay? I never wanted our day to end like this."

"He's fine, ma'am," she reassured the woman. "We're

running a few tests to rule out any broken bones or bleeding internally."

The woman bit back a sob and reached over to take her son's hand. "Oh thank God. I'm so grateful we're all okay."

"Me too, ma'am. Me too." Leilani pulled the resident aside and got the scoop on the three patients in the room before they wheeled the father past the door of the room heading back to trauma bay one, and she excused herself to check in on her patient once more.

While Leilani went over the images, the ultrasound tech performed a cardiac ultrasound and Pam cleaned and bandaged up the lacerations on the man's hand. Of the five passengers in the car, the father seemed to be the one most badly hurt, but the CT had ruled out any fractures in his neck or bleeding in his head, which was great. The man would be sore for sure for a few days, but otherwise should make a full recovery, barring anything abnormal on the cardiac ultrasound.

"Everything looks fine, Doc," the tech said a few minutes later, wiping the gel off the patient's chest. "No abnormalities seen."

"Perfect." Leilani moved aside so they could wheel her portable machine back out of the room. "All right, sir. Looks like you're banged up a bit, but otherwise you'll be fine. I checked on the rest of your family as well, and they're all doing fine too. You all are very lucky."

The daughter, who'd been cleared to move about freely, jumped down and walked over to take her father's hand. Soon, the rest of the family entered to join them in the trauma bay.

"How are you, honey?" the mother asked her husband, kissing his cheek.

"My neck still hurts," he said, then held up his other hand. "And this got messed up a bit. But otherwise, I'm fine." He chuckled. "Remind me never to ride with you again though."

The mother promptly burst into tears and he pulled her down closer to kiss her again.

"I'm kidding," the father said. "You handled that situation better than I would have. I love you so much. It's fine. We're all fine, thanks to you."

Leilani checked the time, then backed out of the room while the family gathered around each other, hugging and laughing and saying prayers of thanks. Tears stung the backs of her eyes, as an unexpected feeling of completeness filled her soul. That's how it should have been for her family all those years ago. It hadn't been, but now at least she'd been able to give that gift of a future to another family. Circle of life indeed.

After finishing up the discharge paperwork for her patients, she checked the time, then discarded her gown and mask into a nearby biohazard bin.

Speaking of futures, it was time to get on with hers.

Holden stood on the beach in front of the Malu Huna Resort as a warm breeze blew and the waves lapped the shore behind him. Joe Kim stood beneath an arbor adorned with palm fronds, tropical flowers and white gauzy fabric that flowed in the wind, ready to marry off his adopted daughter. He'd gotten ordained just for the ceremony. Leilani's mother was passing out leis to the guests as they took their seats. Now all Holden needed was his bride.

He shifted his weight slightly, his bare toes sinking deeper into the sand. His leg hurt less and less these days, thanks to all the outdoor activities available in and around Honolulu. He loved hiking and swimming and had even tried his hand at surfing. The warmer temperatures helped too. And of course, having the woman he loved by his side while he did all those things was the biggest benefit of all. In fact, he'd left his cane inside the hotel today—as he was doing more and more often now. He'd stop and get it though, before the reception, since there would be dancing involved later.

They'd decided on a casual, traditional Hawaiian wedding and he was not upset with it. His white linen pants and shirt were certainly more comfortable than some tuxedo monkey suit, that was for sure. Especially with the great weather. Blue skies, sunshine, a perfect day in paradise.

Hard to believe that a year ago he couldn't wait to get out of this place. Now he couldn't ever imagine calling anywhere else home ever again. He and Leilani had moved into her—now *their*—newly remodeled house three months prior, and things were pretty magical all around as they started their new life together. But even with the great beachfront abode, it wasn't the location so much as the people.

Once they'd told the Kims about their relationship, they had taken him in like a prodigal son. Family like that was something to appreciate and Holden didn't take one day of it for granted.

Same with Leilani. They'd both wanted to go slow, explore their relationship before diving into anything permanent too fast. Given their collective past, it was understandable. But now they were both ready to take the leap.

Holden glanced over and caught sight of his own parents sitting in the first row and flashed them a smile. They'd flown in from Chicago and were loving all Hawaii had to offer. Maybe someday they'd move down here too. He'd like that. As the guests' chairs filled in and the ukulele band they'd hired to play for the ceremony finished a sweet rendition of "Somewhere Over the Rainbow," a hush fell over the crowd. Holden looked up to see his bride at last at the end of the white satin runner covering the aisle of sand between the rows of bow-bedecked folding chairs.

He couldn't stop staring at her, his heart in his throat and his chest swelling with so much love he thought he might burst from the joy of it. She looked amazingly beautiful in a strapless white gown that was fitted on top, then flowed into a silken cloud around her legs, the breeze gently rustling the fabric. Like an angel. His angel, who'd been heaven-sent to teach him how to live and love again, who'd filled his life with so much purpose and meaning and emotion.

The band began "Here Comes the Bride" and the guests stood as Leilani slowly made her way toward Holden, her long dark hair loose beneath the woven crown of flowers on her head and her eyes sparkling with happiness.

She was everything he'd ever dreamed of and nothing he deserved, and his life was infinitely better because she was in it. He planned to tell her as much in his vows. They'd each written their own, but no matter what she said today, it would never mean as much to him as the moment she'd told him she loved him for the first time that day in her hospital room.

Music floated on the jasmine-scented breeze and Leilani reached his side at last.

Before the ceremony began, while the guests were settling into their seats again, Holden leaned closer and whispered for her ears only, "You look spectacular and I'm the luckiest man in the world. I love you, Leilani Kim."

Her smile brightened his entire universe as she beamed up at him. "I'm pretty lucky myself, Holden Ross. I love you too."

He leaned in to kiss her, but Leilani's father cleared his throat. Chuckles erupted from the assembled guests. Holden winked down at his wife-to-be instead, unable to keep the silly, lovesick grin off his face. "Ready to do this thing, Doc?"

"So, so ready," she said, slipping her hand in his as they turned to face her father.

* * * * *

LET'S TALK

Romance

For exclusive extracts, competitions
and special offers, find us online:

f facebook.com/millsandboon

⊙ @millsandboonuk

🐦 @millsandboon

Or get in touch on 0844 844 1351*

For all the latest titles coming soon,
visit millsandboon.co.uk/nextmonth

Want even more
ROMANCE?

Join our bookclub today!

'Mills & Boon books, the perfect way to escape for an hour or so.'

Miss W. Dyer

'Excellent service, promptly delivered and very good subscription choices.'

Miss A. Pearson

'You get fantastic special offers and the chance to get books before they hit the shops'

Mrs V. Hall

Visit millsandbook.co.uk/Bookclub and save on brand new books.

MILLS & BOON